The Broken Door

Joseph B. Galloway

Also by Joseph B. Galloway

Baked Oysters,
A Thanksgiving Reunion

ISBN: 1499151446
ISBN 13: 9781499151442

Cover Design by Ebook Launch

This book is dedicated to my friend Brian Pusateri,
You are closer than a brother.

Acknowledgements

First and foremost, I want to thank God. As we say in Cursillo (at least in Louisiana), the Holy Spirit pinged me and prodded me to finish the book. I want to thank my wife, Charleen, my first reader and critic. Talk about putting her on the spot; "Honey, will you read my book and tell me what you think?" Yeah—right. But she did.

I want to thank editors Anna Sutherland and Jodi Tahsler, and Carol Thoma before them. Their meticulous work forced me to write a better book. Also, early readers Bob Lange and especially Joe Valitchka gave tremendous feedback and detailed suggestions that were invaluable to the story.

And lastly, to the distant and almost anonymous listeners and readers, many of whom are connected to the South Carolina Writers' Workshop: your thoughtful feedback provided focus and motivation beyond what you know.

The Broken Door

One

H e was driving too fast to begin with. Speedometer pushing past 70 on a narrow, curving two-lane country road in the mountains of North Georgia. Top down. Crisp fall afternoon. Lambskin gloves gripping the steering wheel. Toschi Onda driving shoes on the pedals. Steppenwolf's "Born to Be Wild" blaring from the stereo. Invincible fool acting crazy.

Downshifting to navigate a hairpin turn, he miscalculated the physics and strayed too wide. An oncoming truck laden with freshly picked apples swerved to avoid a head-on collision, blaring its horn. He frantically double-clutched into second gear and slammed the brakes as the Basalt Black Porsche 911 Carrera edged off the asphalt. He avoided the truck, but overcompensation spun the car into a pirouette, spewing gravel, coughing smoke, and belching stinky rubber from the screeching tires. The Porsche made three complete turns before it slid back across the road and came to a stop alongside a split-rail fence.

Tommy's heart pounded louder than the bass of the car's stereo. He stared down the lane, unfocused, collecting his wits. The vise-grip he had on the steering wheel squeezed the sweat in the gloves onto the wheel, making them stick a little when he released it. He turned off the engine. Everything went suddenly quiet. He eased his six-foot-two frame out of the car to inspect for damage. No scratches. No dents. No harm. No foul.

Georgia Highway 60 through Dahlonega forks at Camp Wahsega Road before it arcs around on top of the first mountain ridge in the Cohutta National Forest. A canopy of leaves in their full glory of fall color intermingled with the evergreen of pine and hemlock filtering the sunlight. The spent ones let go of their branches and floated on the light breeze. Some landed inside the Porsche.

Tommy peeled off his gloves and tossed them onto the driver's seat. He mopped the sweat off his brow with his forearm and looked around at the scene. He walked up the fence line a ways. A wall of mountain on his left, a sliver of pasture to his right. The fence ended another five hundred feet ahead of him, where a gate opened to a rutted dirt path that crossed the field and began a new ascent up another mountainside. The breeze stirred a whirlpool of brittle leaves around Tommy. His gaze followed the path up a series of switchbacks, winding its way through a stand of trees toward the next ridge. He formed a visor with his hands as the late-afternoon sun beamed an angry glare off the metal roof of what looked to be an old, rickety homestead at the top. *Where am I?* he wondered.

An eighteen-wheeler carrying over five hundred empty chicken cages thundered past as Tommy walked back to the

Porsche. He grabbed his smart phone off the console. A few jabs at its face told him there was no cell service this far into the woods. Tommy reached into the glove compartment for a map. He found his location. *So...I wonder.*

Climbing back into the Porsche, he replaced his gloves and started the engine. The tip of his nose and the lobes of his ears tingled a bit in the late-October nip, but he kept the top down. He plugged his phone into the jack and pulled up a John Mayer song list. The sun sat on top of the mountain, perched next to the house on the distant ridge that seemed vaguely familiar to him. He steered the car back out onto the road and wound his way south.

John Thomas Kennedy, III, enjoyed these jaunts into the mountains. Hard driving on mountain roads was a release for him, especially on tough days. For some reason, this Friday before Halloween was one of those days. Nothing unusual really, but a week's worth of demands from running Kennedy Properties had built up in him like sludge accumulates in the trap of a kitchen-sink drain. This drive was particularly gratifying, intriguing even. *I wonder if I can buy that old place,* he thought as he drove back roads toward Cumming. *Of course I can buy it. I'm Tommy Kennedy.*

Stopped at a red light in front of a Dairy Queen, he saw a disheveled man in a tattered plaid chamois shirt standing on the corner. Instinctively, Tommy pressed a button, and the convertible top eased up and over into place. Another button closed the windows. The spectator was not an old man. He wore dreads. A backpack was at his side. He held a sign—not asking for money, nor offering work in exchange for food. The sign simply read, "Don't be a Stranger." *What the hell's that about?* Tommy thought.

The Porsche turned onto the Atlanta Highway and found GA 400 down to Roswell. It was only 6:30 p.m. Tommy decided to go back to the office. He pulled into the parking lot at Kennedy Square, an office complex of three two-story buildings on Dogwood Road. Founded by his grandfather John Thomas Kennedy, Sr., Kennedy Properties occupied the second floor of the last building. Tommy had no problem finding a space in front of his office.

The buildings formed an L, and a variety of professional businesses rented space at Kennedy Square. Islands of landscaping, mainly azaleas and Bradford Pear trees, dotted the parking lot. In the spring, the trees were an explosion of cotton-white tufts, which offered a nice contrast to the fuchsia of the azaleas. Today, their leaves were a deep crimson.

"Of course. Everyone gone," Tommy scowled as he strode from the reception area to the workroom of cubicles, flipping off light switches. "When are they gonna show some respect?" Across the room, the lights were still on in the offices of his leadership team. "Hey..." Tommy started to say when he stuck his head in Bull's office. "Hmph." Even Bull—Jeff Simpson, Tommy's best friend going back to St. Laurence High School—was absent.

Tommy headed down the hallway toward his office, shedding his jacket and sweater. Out of the corner of his eye, he saw Ellen Krawshen, his CFO, working at her computer. "What's the damn thermostat set on?" he asked, not waiting for a reply. "I want to know what the electric bill is, prorated by each salary."

"Hey. I didn't think you'd be back today," Ellen said. "You left in such a huff." She moved her mouse a bit to the right and clicked.

"All the lights are on, and it's probably 85 degrees in here."

"It got cold this afternoon. The staff asked if we could put the heat on."

"This is only October. If this keeps up, I'll have to dock some pay," Tommy threatened, walking past the admin workroom, where the files were kept, along with the copier and fax machine. He reached in to flip the light switch off. He could hear the hum of an exhaust fan in the restroom across from the kitchen. He cracked open the door, "Anyone in here?" Hearing no reply, Tommy turned off that light, checked the other restroom, and finally made it to his office at the back.

The reception area of Kennedy Properties was welcoming. This was Rosemary Bozeman's domain. She'd worked at Kennedy Properties her entire career, since before Tommy was born. She was aunt and mother to everyone in the office. She wasn't expected to still be at her station after hours.

Her desk of solid maple with walnut veneers tastefully greeted clients and prospects. It was finished in a caramel stain with gold tipping and sat solidly on its rug on top of the marble-tiled floor. A comfortable sofa flanked by two wingback chairs looked across the room at a wall of bookshelves supporting books on the history of Atlanta and the South, as well as various knick-knacks and memorabilia. The workroom adjacent to the reception area was known as "the bull pit." It was outfitted with fit-together desks on carpet-square floors, and three rows of cubicles that had side panels of Office Depot gray-blue fabric.

Tommy's office was well-appointed. An oversized antique oak desk with leather inserts on its surface commanded the middle of the room. A luxurious oriental rug covered the wide-plank hardwood floor. The side walls had wainscoting created from old plantation doors, and the back wall was all glass and looked out over a wild area zoned for green space.

At thirty-eight, Tommy was still the specimen of the college athlete he had been. All of his clothes were custom-made to accommodate his muscular neck and shoulders, which tapered down in a V-shape to his waist. Sandy brown hair with a few errant strands of gray swagged in a slight wave around his ears and down toward his collar. Ellen spied Tommy primping in the mirror as she hovered near his office door, "Kellie called while you were out."

"What'd she want?" Tommy jumped. He tried to play it cool by deftly transitioning into a saunter over to the bar area of his office. A small refrigerator was built into the cabinet, which was stocked with liquors and wines. A variety of glasses sat in a corner hutch that reached up to the ceiling. "And anyway, why are you still here? Who's watching Alex?"

"My mom picked him up from the after-school program," Ellen explained. "I'm meeting someone downtown around seven."

"A date? You have a date?"

"Why shouldn't..." Ellen cleared her throat. "I wouldn't call it a date, necessarily. More like a meet-and-greet." She tucked her thin brown hair behind her right ear.

Tommy poured a scotch and turned to look at Ellen, who stood with arms crossed, looking beneath her glasses at her feet. Her V-neck sweater fit tightly enough to reveal a small muffin-top above the waistline of her slacks. "What'd Kellie want?"

"She wanted to know if you were going to JT's game tonight. She said something about it being the district championship."

"Why didn't she just call me?" Tommy peered at Ellen over the rim of his highball glass.

"She said she tried to call you, but got no answer. She figured you were up in the mountains and had no cell service. So she called me. It was good to catch up with her."

"Hmph," was all Tommy could muster. That his ex-wife and CFO were friendly was a sore spot.

"Anyway, you sure did storm out of here this afternoon. What happened?" Ellen asked.

"I'll tell you Monday, after I've had time to look into a couple of things." Tommy moved to sit behind the desk. A cloud of Clive Christian cologne trailed in his wake. "You get the month-end reports ready?"

"Month-end? Are you looking for those already?"

"Well, it is month-end." Tommy rebooted his computer.

"Oh," Ellen said. The 31st was next Wednesday. She normally needed two days to pull those reports together.

"You can get them to me on Monday," Tommy said. "Shouldn't you be leaving for your date?"

"You really should go to JT's game."

"I know."

"It is his senior year."

"I know."

"District Championship."

"You sound like Kellie. I know. Maybe I will." Tommy took another sip and turned to his computer to check his stock quotes. "Damn!"

A bit later he saw Ellen's office light go out, and then heard the shlock of the front door closing. He glanced up at the wall directly across from his desk. An oversized Bond Street wall clock was the centerpiece of decorative hangings, including a montage of family pictures. He saw JT in a Little League uniform, JT in his eighth grade graduation cap and gown. The aged hands of the clock pointed at gold-leaf Roman numerals that declared the time as 6:50. *I've got time before the game,* he decided. St. Laurence High School was only a few miles from the office.

The eerie quiet was interrupted only by the clock's pendulum. He grabbed the remote to turn on the 42-inch flat-screen TV on the wall above the bar. A stack of messages on the spire at the corner of his desk caught his attention and he pulled them off. At the top was a note in Rosemary's handwriting, "JT's district championship game tonight at 7:30."

Let me just check, Tommy thought as he clicked on Google Earth. He ignored the flashing red light on his phone as he searched the area where he had driven that afternoon. "That's it. I wonder how much land goes with that old house?" He checked a website that gives detail on homes, but he didn't know the address. So, back to Google Earth to get coordinates for the location on Camp Wahsega Road. "Ha!"

He opened a new email and typed a note to Bull:

"Check out this property for me—plat, mortgages, etc. Get back to me Monday."

Fox Business News was on low, but Tommy couldn't really hear it, so engrossed was he in the vision of acquiring the Camp Wahsega property. He pulled a nail file out of the lap drawer and swiveled around to look out the windows on the back wall. Dark outside; he saw only his reflection.

Tommy snapped back to the desk and opened a new email:

"Ellen –

Call Bob over at MWSL Investments and tell him to come over Monday morning to review my accounts. And get a current balance on my bank accounts. Have those along with the month-end reports first thing.

T"

While he was at it, he perused the inbox and answered a few emails. He noticed one from Brother Sean O'Flaherty. *Brother Sean hates using email. I wonder what he wants*, he thought as he opened it.

"Hey, Tommy—Brother Sean here,

Just a quick reminder of our St. Laurence Knights playing for the District Championship tonight. I'm sure you know JT earned All District honors. He'll be recognized before the game. Hope to see you there."

Goosebumps formed on Tommy's arms and neck. He looked at his watch—7:20 p.m. The Bond Street clock corroborated. He clicked the Favorites button on the internet home page. *Can't hurt to take a quick look.* In a few clicks, he found what he was looking for. Tingles ran down his back and up his thighs. His hand moved to his groin. He got up to pour another drink. Back at his desk, he clicked through a few more pages. Bare skin flashing across the screen was more intoxicating than the scotch. He checked his watch again—7:45. *Damn. Shit. I'm too late now.* He perused a couple more scenes.

A loud grumble in his stomach got his attention. He gave into it and turned everything off. *Think I'll head out for a steak.*

Two

Saturday, October 27: Mid-morning

"**H**ey, Tommy. You look like hell," Jessica said as she was leaving Roswell Health Club with little Clare in tow, a yoga mat protruding from her gym bag.

"Daddy! Daddy!" Clare broke loose and ran into Tommy's arms.

He squatted down to catch her, "Hey, sweet pea."

"You get into a fight last night?" Jessica asked. Her flowing, raven-black hair was pulled back into a ponytail that draped down to the middle of her back. An all-weather parka was unzipped over her loose-fitting workout shirt, which camouflaged her perky, athletic body. Yoga pants fit snuggly on her legs.

"Yeah, with one too many scotches," Tommy said with a laugh. He blinked hard a couple of times trying to see through her outfit.

"I'd say more than one too many," Jessica answered. "C'mon, Clare. We have to go home."

"Say, Jess. Remember that Red Cross thing I mentioned?" Tommy asked. "That's tonight. Can you come with me?"

Jessica stared at Tommy a few long moments. She bit the inside of her cheek, eyes and mouth scrunched into a grimace. "You ask me now?" Her hand clenched around a strap of her bag.

"Didn't I mention it a couple of weeks ago?" Tommy flashed his best puppy dog eyes.

"Mention it? I don't remember. Mentioning and asking are two different things."

"C'mon. You can wear that slinky red cocktail dress. I'll be in my tux," Tommy cooed. "We'll do some cha-cha, rub some elbows." Tommy did a little two-step shuffle with Clare in his arms.

"Don't think you're gonna charm me at this late hour," Jessica glared. A couple of guys with racquetball racquets in hand and towels slung over their shoulders walked by and nodded.

"But you're my wife. I should have my beautiful wife on my arm."

"You should've thought that way last year," Jessica said. Last year, Tommy's philandering had gotten him kicked out of his house.

"Don't start that again," Tommy cajoled. "I've apologized. Hell, I went to confession."

"Oh, that makes it alright," Jessica retorted.

"Won't you come with me?" Tommy put Clare down and rubbed his bloodshot eyes.

"It's too late now," Jessica said. "You have to do better than that."

"Better than what?"

"You know what I mean," Jessica said, and she took Clare's hand and left the club. The tang of chlorine-laced antiseptic cleaner hung in the air.

"Damn," Tommy muttered. He turned and headed for the lockers and the healing smell of sweaty socks and used towels.

A billow of hot steam gave Tommy pause before he dragged himself into the spa and found a seat. "Surely I asked Jess a couple of weeks ago."

"What's that?" a voice asked, hidden behind the fog.

"Oh. Nothing. Sorry. Just talking to myself," Tommy apologized. "Maybe I'll call Genevieve's... Nah! That's just the scandal I need—showing up with a paid escort."

"Huh?" The voice asked again.

"Nothing," Tommy repeated. He closed his eyes and slumped back against the wall, practically drowning in his own thoughts and the warm mist.

Saturday, October 27: Evening

Two ruddy valets sprinted to compete for the honor of parking the Basalt Black Porsche 911 Carrera as it pulled into the driveway of the Hyatt Regency Hotel. "Hey, Mr. Kennedy," said the winner, panting as he held the door open for Tommy. Tommy checked his hair in the rear-view mirror. He stuck a $50 bill in the kid's hand as he stepped out in his polished black shoes and crisp pleated shirt. "There's another one of these for you if there are no scratches on her when I leave."

"Yes sir, Mr. Kennedy," said the wide-eyed valet as he climbed into the Porsche, a grin stretching across his face.

Tommy pocketed the parking voucher and donned the coat of his tuxedo. Alderman Johnson and her husband the Reverend Deacon were ahead of him, about to enter the atrium as the bellman held the door. A limousine pulled up and Mayor White emerged with his wife.

"Good evening, Mayor, Mrs. White," Tommy greeted them, extending a hand.

"Tommy Kennedy. How good to see you," Mayor White replied. "You by yourself? Where is your lovely wife, Jessica?"

"I'm sorry to say she couldn't make it tonight," Tommy said. A camera flash shocked them as a question flew at Mayor White.

"Mayor White, what's your stance on the zoning change in favor of the East Metro Atlanta Housing Initiative?"

He ignored the reporter, but Tommy leaned in, "Yeah, I'd like to talk with you about that, Mayor White."

"Not tonight, Tommy. Not tonight," Mayor White said jovially as he took his wife's hand in the crook of his arm and the three of them entered the hotel.

Inside the expansive atrium, sounds of smooth jazz permeated the crowd. Hundreds were milling around tables of exhibits on display for the silent auction portion of the Red Cross Auction and Gala. A California vintner hosted a wine tasting over to the left. Mayor White was hailed over to a small gathering of Atlanta's elite to the right.

"Champagne?" asked a waitress as she shoved a tray full of glasses at Tommy. A multi-tiered fountain in the middle of the atrium glittered with alternating red and white lights.

"No thanks," Tommy said as he spied an old friend at a bar station on the periphery of the action. He made his way through the crowd.

"Scotch, please," Tommy requested of the barkeeper. "With just a splash of water."

"Hey, Tommy," Mike Smith nodded. "Fancy seeing you here." Councilman Mike Smith's district covered portions of west and southwest Atlanta, where many of Kennedy Properties' apartment buildings were located.

"You know, Smitty—see and be seen," Tommy said. "You by yourself?"

"Oh no," Mike replied. "Barb is over gabbing with some Junior League buddies. I'm just taking a break."

A tall drink of water with long blonde hair was standing behind Hap Hampton at one of the auction tables. Hap was a friendly competitor. He and Tommy would sometimes bid against each other on real estate deals. They'd even done a couple of deals together. Tommy winked and raised his glass to the beauty when she glanced his way. "Who's Hap got now?" Tommy wondered aloud. She turned away and led Hap over to another display table—one with jewelry on it.

"Tommy Kennedy!" Brother Sean O'Flaherty came up behind Tommy and slapped a hand on his shoulder, distracting Tommy's voyeuristic musing. When Br. Sean followed Tommy's gaze, he quipped, "Yep. God sure did a good job with that one."

Tommy grinned and turned to shake Br. Sean's hand, "Hey, Brother Sean. You know Councilman Mike Smith?"

"Call me Smitty," Mike said, extending his hand to Br. Sean. "I've heard a lot about you from Tommy."

"Oh? That makes me a little nervous," Br. Sean laughed.

"Can I get you a drink?" Smitty offered.

"I'll have what Tommy's having," Br. Sean said and he turned to Tommy. "We missed you last night."

"I know. I meant to come, but I got caught up in the office," Tommy explained.

Smitty handed the scotch to Br. Sean, "Congratulations. I heard about St. Laurence winning District."

"Yes, we won," Br. Sean said. "JT played magnificently."

"I read that in the paper this morning," Tommy said, looking down at his drink. He dipped a finger in it to stir it.

"Anyway, Tommy, I'd like to visit with you," Br. Sean said. "Can I stop by on Monday?"

"Yeah, sure," Tommy agreed. "Come by anytime. What do you want to talk about?"

"Let's wait till Monday, eh?" Br. Sean said. He saw some parishioners a few tables away and begged his pardon.

Mike Smith grinned. "Uh-oh. Called to the principal's office," he said with a wink.

"Yeah, you're probably right," Tommy smirked. "Hey, Smitty, let me ask you. Are you familiar with the East Metro Atlanta Housing Initiative?"

"Oh man, that's a hot potato," Smitty said with a whistle. "Why do you ask? You have a project on the east side?"

"On the drawing board," Tommy said. "Are you on any committees that deal with that initiative?"

"No. But I've run across some of the players in the past," Smitty said. "Does the East Metro Atlanta Housing Initiative affect your project?"

"I don't think it should," Tommy said. "I got a letter from the Bedrock Foundation seeking information on the development I'm proposing out that way. Our site is further east than where the Bedrock Foundation traditionally operates. I think Alderman Johnson is just fishing." Ms. Alderman and the Reverend Deacon Johnson established the entity under the nonprofit umbrella of his church, the Mount Zion Hill AME Baptist Church.

"Alderman Johnson, huh?" Smitty snorted after taking a sip of his drink. "She used to be on the City Council. But since she lost her seat a few years ago, she's taken on the title of Alderman. I don't think it fools anybody."

"You know her?" Tommy asked. An announcement that the silent auction would end in fifteen minutes came over the loudspeakers.

"Oh yeah. I hear from Ms. Johnson and her husband the good Reverend all the time," Smitty said, not sounding pleased about it.

"Even though your district is on the west side?" Tommy asked.

"The Bedrock Foundation knows no district boundaries," Smitty said. "Their cover is that they help low-income people rent or even acquire property. But they're really a squeeze organization."

"One of those," Tommy said as he raised his glass to take a swallow.

"Yep. You know, they raise a ruckus by making claims of injustice and discrimination, and squeeze funding out of this government agency or that corporation. I'm surprised you haven't run into her before."

"Hmm. I guess my granddad insulated Kennedy Properties pretty well," Tommy said. Another announcement came over the speakers reminding bidders to use their assigned numbers on the silent bid sheets and not their names. A trickle of couples dressed in their gala finery began to file into the ballroom for the seated dinner portion of the event.

"You've been lucky," Smitty said. "Alderman Johnson gets a lot of press support for their 'ministry' work." Smitty's fingers punctuated the word ministry with quotation marks. "I imagine the East Metro Atlanta Housing Initiative—man, that's a mouthful—is a program they'll be able to leverage big time."

"Uh-huh," Tommy said as he watched long gowns with thigh-high slits and furry shoulder wraps enter the ballroom.

"Anyway, good luck with your development," Smitty said. "You better know the players. Let me know if I can help in any way."

"Speaking of players, I need to pay my respects to Lady Shaw," Tommy said, and he took a last gulp of scotch. "Thanks for the info, Smitty. I may take you up on that offer of help."

The crowd began to make their way to their designated tables. Tommy Kennedy was an invited guest of James McKissick, President of the First National Bank, whose table was in the second row behind the lead sponsors. Those tables abutted the dance floor, beyond which was a huge stage set with multiple microphones and amplifiers, music stands and a plethora of brass and wind instruments—enough for at least ten band members. It foretold of the entertainment to come.

FNB's table was still empty, but Mayme Shaw was already seated at the table in front of the bank's. Mayme

Shaw's family was among the early residents of Buckhead as it surged at the turn of the previous century. She was on every important advisory board and involved with all the right charities. Archbishop Hardaway sat to the right of Lady Shaw. Tommy walked right up to Lady Shaw and raised her hand to his lips, "Hello, Mayme. You look ravishing."

"Tommy Kennedy. Don't be so fresh," Mayme said with a twinkle and a smile. Her regal mane of silky-white hair was expertly coiffed. A pearl-handled cane leaned against the table next to her chair. "You look more like Big John every time I see you."

"You are kind to say so."

"And Kellie? Is she with you?" Mayme asked.

"Now, Mayme, you know better than that," Tommy said.

"Oh, of course," Mayme said. "I'm sorry. Please forgive an old woman. And what's your new wife's name? Is she with you?" She spoke with a perfect high-church Southern accent.

"No. Unfortunately, Jessica couldn't come tonight."

"Well, that's a shame," Mayme said. "Have you met the archbishop?"

"No, ma'am."

Mayme pushed back and said, "May I present His Grace, Archbishop Hardaway."

Tommy stepped around Lady Shaw's chair and bowed to the archbishop as he took his hand to kiss his ring, "Your Excellency."

"That's not necessary, Mr. Kennedy," Archbishop Hardaway said as he shook Tommy's hand. "It is a pleasure to meet you."

"Tommy runs Kennedy Properties, Your Grace," Mayme explained. "I was close with his grandfather, John Kennedy."

"How wonderful," Archbishop Hardaway said. He waved Tommy to join them at the table.

"The pleasure is mine, Your Excellency."

Mayme continued, "Kennedy Properties manages hundreds of developments throughout the metro area, and I know Tommy carries on his grandfather's traditions of philanthropy."

"Not hundreds, Mayme," Tommy corrected. "We only have dozens of properties."

"Well, dozens, then," Mayme said. "Hundreds of tenants."

"Yes, ma'am. Many hundreds of those."

"That sounds like fine work, Mr. Kennedy," Archbishop Hardaway said. "In what parish do you live?"

"I live up in Roswell and attend St. Laurence."

"And Tommy has just joined the board of Catholic Charities," Mayme said.

"That's splendid, Mr. Kennedy," Archbishop Hardaway said. "We do so appreciate all your good efforts and support."

"It's an honor," Tommy said. "And besides, you probably know how hard it is to say no to Mayme Shaw."

"That I do, Mr. Kennedy. That I do."

"Oh, stop it," Mayme said. She sat a little straighter and higher in her chair. "I told John Kennedy years ago that I'd look out for his grandson. Since many of the Kennedy Properties locations are in areas where the works of Catholic Charities are vital, I thought we'd be a good fit for Tommy. We asked him to join the board, and he agreed."

"Well, you're right, Mayme," Tommy said. "I've been a little slack in picking up where Big John left off. I'm glad you asked and look forward to getting involved."

Tables were filling up fast. The wait staff began to fill tea glasses and take drink orders.

"I have some particular points of interest on where I think you can be the most effective at Catholic Charities," Mayme said. "You should come for lunch."

"Yes, ma'am, I would love that," Tommy agreed. Salad plates were distributed around the table. Tommy took his cue and rose to leave. "May I call you next week to arrange a visit?"

"I will count on it," Mayme said, extending her hand.

After shaking Lady Shaw's hand, Tommy turned to bow, "Your Excellency."

The music on the PA system was a tad too loud. Mixed with the clatter of dinnerware and the general din of conversation, it was difficult to talk with tablemates except to those sitting very near. That suited Tommy just fine. He sat next to his banker, James McKissick. The two seats on Tommy's other side were still empty.

"Whose seats are those?" Tommy inquired.

"I asked Hap Hampton to join us this evening," James said. "I know you two do some projects together."

Tommy saw Hap's beautiful escort approaching. Talk about a near occasion of sin. He rose to greet them, as did James McKissick.

"Hey, Tommy, ole buddy," boomed Hap, a bear of a big man with a balding pate. Hap played O-line for the University of Georgia. "Y'all, this is Heather." They shook hands all around and sat. A waiter asked for drink orders. Heather ordered a piña colada. All that blonde hair fell in tresses down her spine; her dress was cut so low that Tommy could see the dimples in the small of her back. He asked for another scotch.

James McKissick leaned over to Tommy, "Any progress on your east-side project?"

"Progress? Some progress," Tommy said. "You guys interested in providing financing?"

"Could be," James shrugged. "We could stand to have some exposure on the east side. Good for our CRA score." CRA stood for Community Reinvestment Act. Banks must demonstrate a certain amount of business in what are deemed to be low-income areas of town.

"I thought real estate loans have caused a lot of trouble for banks," Tommy said. "FNB not caught up in that?"

"We've had our share of challenges," President McKissick admitted. "But our relationship with Kennedy Properties is golden. You've always maintained strong equity and have never been late on any payments. Well, not since you've run the company."

Overhearing, Hap bellowed, "Hey Tommy, I was just talking with Alderman Johnson earlier tonight. She asked me if I partnered any with Kennedy Properties."

"She did, did she?" Tommy asked as he took a glass of scotch from a waiter. "I wonder why she would think to ask something like that?"

"Yeah, it seemed a little strange. I'm sure she knew the answer before she asked," Hap said. As the salad plates were already on the table, the guests began their meal. Tommy enjoyed the view as Heather's already low-cut neckline gaped when she leaned to the table's center for a cruet.

"Hey, baby," Hap intervened. "Just ask and I'll get it for you." Hap reached for the salt and pepper to season his salad. He continued, "You know she and her husband are all over that East Metro Atlanta Housing Initiative."

"That's what I heard tonight," Tommy said.

"Hey, man, you know I've got some properties over on that side of town. I've worked with the Reverend Deacon and Alderman Johnson before. Maybe we should talk." Hap finished his salad between sentences and began to pick at Heather's salad plate. He waved the waiter over to order more drinks.

"It'd be good to have some experience in navigating the political potholes," James offered. A hoard of servers descended on the floor—some taking salad plates away, others bringing the main course.

"James, you got any branches on the east side?" Hap asked.

"No, and we have only a few loans out that way," James said.

"Maybe Tommy and I could add a space for a new FNB branch on this project," Hap said. "That'll get your CRA rating up."

"We could talk more about that," James said.

"And with a branch, Alderman Johnson might loosen up," Hap said. "This could all work real good."

Tommy slammed back his scotch. A slow churn rumbled in the pit of his stomach.

After allowing time for dinner to progress to dessert, the auctioneer took his place on stage, his spotters located strategically around the ballroom. The Red Cross Auction and Gala got going in full swing. An hour past the unseasoned chicken and cold roasted potatoes, Tommy made his excuses, slipped out of the hall, and went home.

Three

Monday, October 29: Morning

The last work week in October began with a cold drizzle. Tommy slammed a dripping umbrella into a bucket-stand by the front door. A little after 9 a.m., the lobby was already abuzz with ringing phones and waiting people.

"Kennedy Properties, this is Rosemary. How may I direct your call?" Rosemary Bozeman, receptionist emeritus, the voice of Kennedy Properties, spoke with grace and charm. Her thick black hair salted with gray strands generously interspersed throughout was pulled back into a bun. Wire-frame glasses allowed her steely blue eyes to watch over the office like a hawk. The size of a ballerina, she executed a turn with perfect fluidity as she juggled the phone with the stack of messages she held out for Tommy as he breezed past.

"Good morning, Mr. Kennedy," a meek voice rose from the bull pit.

Tommy poked his head inside Ellen's office, "You got those reports ready?"

24

"I'll have them in a bit," Ellen said. "You normally don't want them until the last day of the month."

"Well, I want them today," Tommy said as he made his way to his office. He stripped off his Burberry coat and threw it across a high-back chair in front of his massive desk. A press of a button on the remote brought CNBC to life. He thumbed through the stack of messages and noticed a call from Mike Smith.

Rosemary walked in with his cup of coffee just the way he liked it, a drop of cream and no sugar. "A Mr. Brown is here to see you, as is Bob Clarke." She retrieved his coat and hung it in the closet.

"Who is Mr. Brown?" Tommy asked, cradling the hot mug in both hands.

"Mr. Brown is President of the South Towers Tenants Association," Rosemary said, identifying one of Kennedy Properties' assets. "Did you see JT play Friday night?"

Tommy didn't answer. He just raised the cup under his nose to draw in a long whiff of steaming coffee.

Rosemary slammed her hands on her hips and stared.

"Please don't start in on me. Where's Bull?" Tommy inquired after the whereabouts of his property manager.

"He isn't in yet," Rosemary said. "And anyway, Mr. Brown said he was here specifically to see you."

"Great. Well, have him wait. I need to return Councilman Smith's call," Tommy said, dismissing Rosemary as he reached for the phone.

"Councilman Smith's office."

"May I speak to the good Councilman?" Tommy asked.

"Just a minute. May I tell him who's calling?"

"Tommy Kennedy returning his call."

"Just a moment." Muzak kicked in with a symphonic version of "I'm a Believer."

Tommy took a sip of coffee and noticed a headline flash on the TV screen about the upcoming stress test on the twenty largest commercial banks in the country. He reached for the remote to increase the volume when Councilman Smith came on the line. "Hey, Tommy, how are you this morning?"

"Good, Smitty. You?"

"Just fine," Smitty said. "How much did you spend Saturday night?"

"Not too much," Tommy said. "I donated a week's stay at my beach condo, but I didn't wait around to see how much it went for. How'd you fare?"

"I don't even know," Smitty said. "When Barb gets with her friends at those auction events, I just hope and pray that we can pay the bills the next week."

"I hear you," Tommy chuckled. "Hey, I've got a Mr. Brown from the South Towers property in my lobby."

"Yeah, I was calling to give you a heads-up about that," Smitty said.

"You know why he's here?" Tommy asked.

"Probably," Smitty said. "You know that South Towers is in my district. Mr. Brown called on my office last week complaining about your manager and feeling like their concerns are not being heard."

"Why didn't you mention this to me Saturday night?" Tommy would have appreciated more of a heads-up. He tried to avoid conflict when possible.

"Didn't seem to be the right opportunity. And then the conversation veered toward the East Metro Atlanta Housing Initiative."

"Yeah, that," Tommy said.

"Anyway, Tommy. Since Mr. Brown is a constituent, we told him we'd talk with you," Smitty said.

"Well—what did he complain about?" Tommy asked.

"The usual stuff, mostly," Smitty said. "Leaky faucets, unkept grounds, and now with this cold snap, they're worried about the heating."

"I can have Bull check into those things," Tommy said.

"That's another thing," Smitty said.

"Huh?"

"Mr. Brown complained about Jeff Simpson. Said he was rude and dismissive," Smitty said.

"Bull? Rude?" Tommy repeated. "He didn't get that nickname for being meek and mild. And I need someone with girth and force to deal with those people."

"C'mon, Tommy. Those people are citizens, my constituents," Smitty said. "When tenants complain of maintenance issues, that's an easy fix we can all work on. But can't your man be a little more professional?"

A short pause allowed for another sip of coffee. "Tell you what, Councilman," Tommy said. "I'll tell Mr. Brown that you and I talked this morning and that I'll discuss his issues with my property manager and see what we can do. That should get you more votes next election."

"That'd be good," Smitty said.

"And, can you pull any sway with Alderman Johnson?" Tommy asked.

"You know she's not in my district," Smitty said.

"I know. But, if you could get me some sense of her hot buttons, then I might be able to avoid partnering with Hap Hampton on this new east-side project," Tommy said.

"You and Hap have some partnerships already, don't you?" Smitty asked.

"Yeah, but I'd rather have less of them with that Bulldog," Tommy said, bringing up an old school rivalry.

"You Yellow Jackets just get all snooty," Smitty said.

"Hah! That's because we have higher SAT scores than they do," Tommy said.

"Speaking of Yellow Jackets," Smitty said, "you think you could get a swarm of them together for a little fundraiser I'm having?"

Tommy ended the call after a few more minutes of negotiating information and support. He swiveled around to watch the rain pelt his windows as he finished his coffee. He turned to press Rosemary's extension, "Send Bob back to see me."

Bob Clarke, Vice President of MWSL Investments, walked in on shiny wingtips, a bold red tie tucked inside his buttoned-up pinstriped suit, briefcase in hand. "Hello, Tommy. How are you this morning?"

"Bob, thanks for coming on such short notice," Tommy met him at his office door with hand extended. "I'm thinking of buying a mountain property, so I need a quick update on my accounts and how much cash I have available." Tommy directed Bob to sit on the leather sofa across from the TV and bar area. Tommy turned a high-back chair at his desk around to join him.

"I have it all right here," Bob said as he placed his briefcase on the coffee table. "You learn anything on that show?" he asked, pointing at the flat-screen.

"What? CNBC?" Tommy said. "Just background noise."

Bob retrieved a couple of folders from his case, "Are you looking at the Kennedy Properties account, or are you thinking personal investment?"

"I'm not sure yet," Tommy answered. "Probably a personal acquisition. I might like to have a mountain getaway. How much cash is in there?"

After a quick review of balances and returns, Tommy asked, "Is that all I'm getting? Hell, I can do better lending my money to Kennedy Properties."

"Hold on a minute," Bob said. "You have to remember you've instructed me that you need to have cash available at all times, and that you don't want to see any negative results on your statements."

"Yeah, but I need to get more than three percent," Tommy complained.

"In this environment, three percent is good." Bob held his ground. "What is James McKissick paying you on your deposits over at FNB?"

"I know. But still." Tommy stared blankly at the statement Bob had given him.

"If you'd let me diversify your holdings as we've discussed, we could do better," Bob said. "And we could attach a line of credit to your account should you need cash at a time when selling something might not be the best thing at the moment."

"Yeah. Yeah. You've told me that before," Tommy said. "But we've got the election coming and the fiscal cliff looming."

Bob raised his hand to deflect those concerns. "You need to turn off that TV," he suggested.

Tommy walked Bob to his office door to bid him good-bye. "I'll let you know what I need. Thanks for coming by." He then called down the hallway for Ellen to join him.

As Ellen entered, Tommy's phone buzzed.

"Mr. Brown is still here," Rosemary reminded him.

Tommy waved Ellen off, "Give me a few more minutes."

Rosemary showed Mr. Brown to Tommy's office. Tommy rose to greet him and offered him a seat on the sofa. "Get you more coffee, Mr. Brown?"

"No thank you, I'm fine," Mr. Brown said.

"Please have a seat," Tommy invited.

"I prefer to stand."

"Okay then," Tommy said.

"Mr. Kennedy," Mr. Brown began. He stood behind the sofa and Tommy leaned against the side of his desk, arms folded. "I represent the South Towers Tenants Association, and we have some concerns, not the least of which is with your Mr. Simpson."

"I wish..."

"I've called your office many times and left messages for you, but have gotten no response," Mr. Brown continued. "I had no alternative but to call on Councilman Mike Smith's office for help."

Tommy raised both his hands in a sign of surrender, "I spoke with Councilman Smith this morning, Mr. Brown. Won't you please sit down?"

Mr. Brown plowed ahead, "Mr. Kennedy, we at South Towers have complained for months about the leaky roof, plumbing issues, and the unkept grounds."

"I know, Mr. Brown," Tommy said, still standing with Mr. Brown now at the end of the sofa closest to the desk.

"Councilman Smith shared your concerns with me. I will personally see that we look into every one of them."

"Mr. Kennedy, don't you dare just dismiss me," Mr. Brown said.

"No sir, Mr. Brown," Tommy assured him, trying to keep a level tone and not let his annoyance creep through. "I assure you we will look into your issues." Tommy moved around his desk to call Rosemary on her extension, "Please bring me the South Towers file."

Rosemary carried in a large accordion file and pulled out the maintenance folder. She stood there, peering down her nose, watching Tommy peruse the information. "Yes?" he asked her. Rosemary said nothing, and turned on her heel to leave the office.

Tommy spread open the file on his desk, "I see here in the file notations of trips by our maintenance team out to South Towers."

"That's interesting, Mr. Kennedy," Mr. Brown said. "I haven't seen any maintenance teams out at South Towers. And may I ask when is the last time you were out at South Towers, Mr. Kennedy?"

Tommy closed the folder and walked toward the door. "Mr. Brown, I give you my word that we will address all your concerns. I will speak with Mr. Simpson this morning."

Mr. Brown didn't move from Tommy's desk, "And about Mr. Simpson. He has totally ignored our requests. He has treated us with disdain and disrespect. We cannot abide that."

"I understand, Mr. Brown," Tommy said. "I will fix that from this moment on."

"We don't want to deal with Mr. Simpson anymore," Mr. Brown said.

"Mr. Simpson is Vice President of Property Management," Tommy explained. "He's been with Kennedy Properties for over ten years."

"That's all fine and good for Kennedy Properties," Mr. Brown said, "but he hasn't worked on South Towers at all."

"I will get with Mr. Simpson and we'll address all your concerns," Tommy said again. He held the door to his office open and ushered Mr. Brown to the lobby.

"And what assurances can I have?" Mr. Brown asked.

"You have my word, Mr. Brown," Tommy said.

Mr. Brown's direct stare was so intense that Tommy didn't notice Rosemary standing with toe tapping, also staring at Tommy over her wire-frame glasses, until Mr. Brown left. "What?"

Rosemary just shook her head. A vein visibly pulsated on her forehead.

"Say what you're gonna say," Tommy said. He headed back to his office and Rosemary followed.

"Your grandfather built South Towers," Rosemary began. "It was the biggest project of Kennedy Properties at the time."

"I know that," Tommy said.

"That was a big gamble to take in the mid-60's," Rosemary continued. "John Kennedy was one of the first developers to cater to the south side. That's when Mayme Shaw began to back your grandfather's business."

"I didn't know that," Tommy said.

"She recognized the good thing he was doing for our community. He built those properties for people to live comfortable lives in. Don't you forget that!"

Tommy picked up his coffee cup from his desk and found it empty. Rosemary grabbed the cup from his hand and left the office.

"Ellen!" Tommy yelled as his cell phone vibrated. It was Bull. "Bull, where are you?" Ellen appeared in the doorway and Rosemary came up behind her with a fresh cup of coffee. Tommy waved them in.

"I'm over at the Kennedy Lakes Country Club clubhouse," Bull said. Kennedy Lakes was the stalled upscale development on the northwest side of town.

"What is it now?" Tommy asked, exasperation creeping into his voice. Ellen took her seat in one of the high-back chairs. She held a folio on her lap and placed her coffee mug on the massive desk in front of her.

"Nothing new. Just a couple of contractors to check on," Bull said.

"Well, get in here as soon as you can," Tommy said. "I just had a rather tense meeting with Mr. Brown of South Towers. Smitty even called to warn me about him this morning. People are not happy out there."

"I can tell you what's going on with that," Bull said.

"Save it for when you get here," Tommy said, cutting him off. "And I have another property I want you to check on." Tommy pressed "end" and focused on the spreadsheets Ellen placed in front of him. "How was your date?"

"Oh, it was..." Ellen began before catching herself. "I told you it wasn't a real date. Besides, I don't have time for a relationship."

"What? I don't demand all your spare time, do I?" Tommy said as he flipped through the reports. "Why are our delinquencies so high? What are our property relations people doing?"

"They're on the phone constantly," Ellen defended them. "You should hear some of their stories."

"I don't want to hear any stories," Tommy said.

"So many unemployed or underemployed," Ellen said.

"Waah, waah," Tommy turned a page. "Their job is to collect the rents. Look at how Bull has maintenance expenses under control." The phone rang, and Tommy picked it up.

Ellen couldn't hear who it was, but she guessed it was a tenant representative.

"Yes, but..." Tommy said. Ellen sat back in her chair, crossed her legs, and pushed her glasses up her nose.

"I know, but..." he tried to break in. Ellen took a sip from her mug.

"Okay, I will," and he hung up and looked blankly past Ellen. He then punched Rosemary's extension, "How'd that call get through?"

"I was—uh—away from my desk," Rosemary said.

"I pay you to control the incoming..." and the phone clicked. He held the receiver out from his ear and stared at it before replacing it in its catch.

"So?" He refocused on Ellen's spreadsheets.

"Don't the maintenance expenses look below trend to you?" Ellen asked.

"It's that kind of expense control that'll get my profit margin back up. Bull's outsourcing the mechanics and the techs was a brilliant move. That reduced our headcount by twelve. Can we outsource collections?"

"Hmm...I guess anything's possible. But we run a pretty tight ship," Ellen said. "You know how we've scrutinized every expense since the crash of 2008."

"There must be some areas of opportunity," Tommy said. "What do we have to do to get profit margins back to 2005 levels? What's the utility bill? Damn, it was hot in here Friday afternoon. And what about benefits costs?"

"What about them?"

"Isn't it time to get new bids on our health insurance?" Tommy asked.

"We can do that," Ellen said slowly. "But you know those premiums go up every year."

"Yeah, and don't we pay the entire premium for everyone?"

"Yes, we do."

"Could we pay just the employee cost and let them pay for their family coverage?" Tommy wondered.

Ellen hesitated a moment. Then quietly, she said, "That could put a significant burden on some of our people."

"Burden. Hell, they should be glad they have a job, much less health insurance." Tommy took a swallow of coffee. "Put out for bids and allocate the family cost to the employees. Let's see what that does to the bottom line."

Eyes wide behind her glasses, Ellen just looked at Tommy.

"What?"

"Nothing," Ellen said. After reviewing the changes on the Cash Balance statement, Ellen stood up.

"What's his name?" Tommy asked.

"Who?"

"Your date Friday night."

She ignored the question and turned to leave his office, folio tucked under her arm. She stopped midway and turned around to ask, "I know it's a month away, but will we close the office the day after Thanksgiving?"

"Huh?"

"People will need some advance notice if they want to make plans with their families," Ellen said.

"Again this year?" Tommy stammered. "We go through this every year. Friday is a workday just like any other day. Why should we be closed?" He wadded up a piece of paper and slammed it into the wastebasket. "If those people want the Friday after Thanksgiving off, they should increase their production, get their collection rates up, handle tenant relations better—and keep the thermostat below sixty-eight!"

Ellen had already exited his office and closed the door behind her, but Tommy's rant penetrated the walls and chased after her. She crossed paths with one of the property relations staff in the hallway. Their eyes met in a knowing roll. Ellen ducked into the restroom to splash some water on her face. She gawked at the tired circles under the eyes in the mirror staring back at her.

Monday, October 29: Late morning

Tommy stood behind his desk, pressed his fingers against his eyes, and then ran them across his forehead and down his cheeks as he drew in a deep breath. He exhaled slowly and stared at the TV, not really seeing the headlines, much less listening to the policy wonks debate the upcoming election's impact on the markets. He drained his coffee mug, sat back down, picked up the receiver and punched buttons to call Councilwoman Wilcox.

He rolled his eyes when he heard the greeting: "It's a great day in Roswell." This was Councilwoman Virginia Wilcox's stamp of enthusiasm on the face of local politics.

"May I speak with Councilwoman Wilcox?" Tommy asked.

"I'm sorry, but she is out of the office," said the receptionist cheerfully. "May I take a message?"

"Yes. Please have her call Tommy Kennedy," he said as Bull barged into his office and plopped down. His stoutness challenged the chair's capacity. He pulled a bandana out of his pocket to wipe his clean-shaven head as he waited for Tommy to hang up.

"Let me tell you about South Towers," Bull began, but Tommy held up his hand to stop him.

"I need you to look up a property for me," Tommy said. "Find out who owns it, what they owe, and the general scoop, as usual."

"Sure, Boss. What's the address?" Bull folded the rag and tucked it in his back pocket.

"44 Camp Wahsega Road," Tommy told him.

"44, eh?" Bull said. "That's a great number."

"Yeah. Yeah. I knew you'd get a kick out of that," Tommy said.

Forty-four had been Bull's number in high school. Back in the day, St. Laurence's number 44 could flatten a defensive end better than any fullback in the district.

"Where the hell is Camp Wahsega Road?" Bull asked.

"It's up above Dahlonega in the Cohutta National Forest."

"I thought you wanted something up in Highlands."

"Hey, well, you never know. Just find out who owns it," Tommy said.

Bull stood to leave, but just then Brother Sean O'Flaherty stuck his head in the office, "Well, well, well. If it isn't my old one-two punch." Br. Sean stood in the doorway dressed in his standard Christian Brother's garb of a blue buttoned-down Oxford shirt and khaki pants. He had on a wool herringbone jacket and held his hat in his hand. His thin, graying wisps of hair were groomed straight back.

"Hey Coach," Bull shouted. He grabbed Br. Sean's hand with both of his in a powerful greeting. "I was just reminding Tommy how great we were back in high school."

"Boy, when I called a 44 power," Br. Sean reminisced, "you two would steamroll the poor defensive tackle and jam up the entire inside of the line."

"Nobody could stop us," Bull remembered.

"I still say we should have thrown more—to me, of course," Tommy said.

"How often did we throw the tight-end drop pass off that 44 power?" Br. Sean asked.

"Not enough," Tommy said as he slapped Br. Sean on the shoulder.

Bull pounded the desk in a hearty chuckle, "You guys excuse me. I've got a couple of things to check on," he said as he took his leave. "Great to see you, Coach." He headed out of the office and down the hall.

"That Jeff is something else," Br. Sean said. "How long has he been working at Kennedy Properties?"

"Geez, Brother Sean. Something like ten years now," Tommy said. "I think he came onboard the year my father died."

"You've been friends a long time," Br. Sean commented.

"Bull's a good guy," Tommy said. "He takes care of things for me."

"Hey. Whataya say we go grab a bite for lunch?" Br. Sean said. "My treat."

"Go out in this rain?" Tommy said. He turned to see that the rain was now hardly more than a drizzle. "Well, okay. But I'm buying. I insist."

"If you say so, my boy." Br. Sean followed Tommy out of the office.

When they reached the lobby, Rosemary informed him, "Councilwoman Wilcox returned your call."

"Damn. I wish I'd caught her," Tommy said. "Oh. Excuse my language, Brother Sean."

"Ginny Wilcox is such a fine lady, and good for Roswell," Br. Sean said. "Wasn't she in your class?"

"I think she was three or four years behind me, Brother Sean," Tommy said as he drew his umbrella from out of the bucket and held the door for Br. Sean.

"Ah. How those years all run together now," Br. Sean said.

"Going to lunch," Tommy yelled back at the lobby.

Four

Monday, October 29: Lunchtime

"Tell me how it's really going," Br. Sean asked after the waitress brought their sweet tea and took their orders. They sat in a booth against the far wall of the Azalea Grille. A Garth Brooks tune played from the jukebox.

"It's going great," Tommy said. "I was just reviewing our financials with my CFO this morning."

"I read about you all the time in the newspaper," Br. Sean said. "You have a lot of projects on the drawing board."

"Yes, sir, we do," Tommy agreed. "We gotta grow. Seems I remember learning that you're either moving forward or going backward; there is no standing still." Tommy grinned at Br. Sean.

"I may have said that a time or two in the locker room," Br. Sean admitted, "but I was talking more about life in general, improving as a player and as a man, or otherwise, backsliding. And anyway, I always knew you'd do well in whatever business you chose. You were such a good student and athlete."

"This is a fun business...most of the time," Tommy said. "But lately, it's a little consuming."

"A little consuming?" Br. Sean repeated. "I've hardly seen you in the stands this season."

"I know. I know." Tommy looked away from Br. Sean over the tables and to the back toward the kitchen. Through coats of grease painted on the window that separated the kitchen from the counter area, he could see frantic cutting, spooning, and flipping. A torrent of thick fog from bacon burgers and French fries wafted out every time the kitchen door swung open.

"Think of how important St. Laurence football was to you back then," Br. Sean reminded him. "How hard we worked. How rewarding it was to go so far in the playoffs. Strong bonds of friendship were forged that have lasted until this very day. Look at you and Jeff."

Tommy knew the camaraderie that was built through all the sacrifice of blood, sweat, and tears on the practice field and in the weight room.

"It's like that for JT," Br. Sean said. "You should be a part of that."

"I'm not sure JT wants me around," Tommy said.

"Why would you say that?"

"I didn't want my dad around."

"My boy, don't be so thick. You are not like your dad," Br. Sean said. "I know that football was your refuge, a way for you to be a part of something like a family, a replacement for what you didn't have at home. And I know what an ass your father was, God rest his soul. But you are not your father. You're better than that." The click of the jukebox changing records snapped sharply over the low rumble of a room full of diners.

Br. Sean continued, "JT wants you at the games. He says it doesn't matter to him. But I see him looking around the stands for you. And I know Kellie wants you there, too."

"Kellie called me Friday," Tommy said.

"Yes, and so did I. I even sent you an email," Br. Sean reminded him.

"I saw that," Tommy admitted.

"You know I loathe using email," Br. Sean said. He took a sip of tea, then asked, "Where is Jessica on all this?"

"What do you mean where is Jessica on this?" Tommy's fist squeezed his napkin into a ball. "Leave Jessica out of this."

"Forgive me for asking, but is she keeping you from your son?" Br. Sean asked pointedly.

"No, she wouldn't do that. In fact, she used to check with Kellie for the schedule and leave me post-it notes on the fridge."

"Used to?" Br. Sean's eyebrows rose.

Tommy looked at Br. Sean, perplexed. Surely he had told him of their separation.

"Not anymore?" Br. Sean dug. "What about this season?"

"Well," Tommy wiped the accumulated condensation from the tea glass off the table in front of him. "Jess and I are separated right now."

"Oh, my goodness, my boy," Br. Sean said.

"I thought you knew," Tommy said. He hated feeling like he let Br. Sean down.

The waitress walked up just then, balancing a tray of lunch plates and a pitcher full of tea. "Who had the club?"

Tommy raised his hand. A stack of turkey supported strips of bacon poking out from the bottom half. Above it, ham was piled high on the second layer of the double-tiered sandwich. Avocado oozed over the edges, fighting against the toothpicks that were desperately trying to hold it all together. French fries dribbled from the plate onto the table. A similarly over-stuffed pastrami on rye, with melted Swiss lapping at the crust, went to Br. Sean. A heaping plate of onion rings was placed between them for good measure.

After the waitress refilled their glasses with more sweet tea, she barked, "Y'all need anything else?"

"No thanks," Tommy said, grabbing a fry and shoving it into his mouth.

Br. Sean crossed himself and began to pray.

"Oh, yeah," Tommy said, wiping his hand on a napkin as he crossed himself and joined in the prayer.

After coaxing some catsup out of the bottle, Br. Sean got back to business. "Listen to me, my boy. JT looks up to you. He wants to be like you. Of course, he's got big shoes to fill at St. Laurence."

"Hmph," Tommy grunted out of a mouth full of club sandwich.

"You know he has a real shot at a college scholarship."

"Yeah."

"Shouldn't you be around for all that hoopla?" Br. Sean asked. "Aren't you proud?"

"Of course, I'm proud," Tommy said.

"Well, why don't you show it?" Br. Sean asked.

Councilwoman Ginny Wilcox stopped by their table, "Hello, Brother Sean, Tommy." She laid her hand on Tommy's shoulder and ran it down to his tricep and squeezed gently. Brown bangs cut across her eyebrows, accenting the bob that fell to her shoulders. Her blue blazer was tailored to accentuate the fullness of the womanly curves that filled it. "Tommy, I returned your call this morning." Her hand lingered on his arm.

"I know, Ginny. Thank you," Tommy said.

"Don't let me interrupt your lunch," Ginny said. "I just saw you two over here and wanted to say hello."

"So glad you did, Councilwoman," Br. Sean said.

"Hey. How about those Knights?" Ginny said with a wink.

"Yes, we're in the playoffs. Praise God," Br. Sean said.

"I'll be in the office this afternoon, Tommy," Ginny said. "Call me back." She took her leave and stopped to greet a couple other constituents a few tables over.

Their waitress refilled their glasses and picked the empty onion ring plate off the table. "Y'all save some room for desert?"

"No thanks," Tommy said. "Just the check."

They climbed into Tommy's Porsche to ride back to the office. "Fine car," Br. Sean said. "Business must be good."

Tommy paid no heed as he turned the key in the ignition.

"Tommy, my boy. Listen. I need your help."

"What do you need, Brother Sean?" Tommy revved the 911 Carrera before shifting into gear.

"You remember the service project St. Laurence High does every Thanksgiving? We need a sponsor this year."

"What happened to Oubre Chevrolet?" Tommy asked.

"Steve had to pull out this year," Br. Sean said. "And anyway, he's been our lead sponsor for five years. We can't let him monopolize all the good works."

"Hah!" Tommy said. "Chevy sales must be down."

"I wouldn't know about that," Br. Sean said. "What do you say? Can I count on you?"

"What'll I have to do?" Tommy asked.

"It would be great if you would help us serve the dinner. It's the Saturday after Thanksgiving, hopefully right after practice if we win the Quarterfinals. It'll be a great activity for you and JT to do together."

"I'll see," Tommy said.

"And of course, we need you to cover the cost," Br. Sean said.

"Of course. How much is that?"

"It runs about $25 per family fed. Piggly Wiggly gives us food at just over their cost. Last year, we served about three hundred families."

"That's seventy-five hundred bucks!" Tommy said.

"We could give you lead sponsor billing for $5000," Br. Sean said.

"I'll check with our CFO and see what our charity budget is," Tommy said.

"But then I'd have to get the rest of the funding from other donors," Br. Sean thought out loud. "We could do that. We've done it before."

"We'll see," Tommy said again as they pulled into Kennedy Properties' parking lot.

"Thanks for lunch, Tommy my boy," Br. Sean said. They shook hands and parted ways underneath a cloudy sky.

"Always something," Tommy muttered under his breath. He chuckled to himself as he watched the strong breeze push at Br. Sean's back, causing a few errant strands of Vitalisized hair to stand up on his head before he corralled them under his hat.

Monday, October 29: Afternoon

Gray clouds rushed by as if running scared from a demon. At least the rain had stopped. Tommy opened the door to Kennedy Properties and had to lunge after it—the gale-force wind almost slammed it against the wall.

"How was lunch?" Rosemary asked as Tommy replaced the umbrella in the bucket.

"Everybody wants something," Tommy complained. "Where's Bull?"

"He should be in his office," Rosemary said. She rewrapped her abundant salt-and-pepper hair into a new bun.

Tommy walked through the bank of cubicles on his way to Bull's office. "Hello, Mr. Kennedy." "Good afternoon, Mr. Kennedy."

Tommy heard the greetings, as well as the tapping of keys on adding machines and calculators. *The sound of money*, he thought. A few phone conversations were in progress. One, "Yes, I hear you, and I'm sorry. But you're fourteen days late." Another..."Thank you for your call. I'll pass that along to our maintenance staff." The crinkling sound of paper being wadded into a ball followed close behind.

A third conversation was more heated, "I don't care. You've breached our agreement. I'll have to turn you over to a collection agent." Tommy stuck his head into that cubicle and gave a thumbs-up.

A few steps further, and he found Bull sitting at his desk, a McDonald's bag spread flat with French fries poured out and a half-eaten Big Mac in his hand—the other half apparently in his mouth.

"Hey, Boss," Bull said. He sucked on the straw sticking out of the super-sized Coke.

"Were you able to find out anything about my mountain property?" Tommy asked, stealing a fry.

"You sound like it's already yours," Bull said.

"Yeah, I think I'm gonna buy it," Tommy said.

"What? Sight unseen?" Bull asked as he crammed another bite of Big Mac into his mouth.

"Don't worry about that," Tommy said. "What'd you find out?"

"I went to the county records site and found out that a Mr. Christopher McCarter owns the property. He's had it since the 40's. I didn't see any liens on it or anything."

"What about size?"

With the last of the Big Mac shoved in his mouth, Bull answered, "Dahum aries look showerd froma..."

Tommy stopped him, "You eat like a pig."

After a swig of Coke to wash down the burger, Bull said, "The boundaries look to go down from the road to the bottom of the ravine and halfway up another mountain—about thirty acres in all."

"How much road frontage?" Tommy asked as his cell phone vibrated. He took the call, "Hey, Jess."

"Hi, Tommy. Am I interrupting anything?" Jessica asked.

"No, not really," Tommy said. "I'm in Bull's office going over a few things. What's up?" Bull took the opportunity to polish off the fries.

"Time has snuck up on me. I can't believe that Wednesday is Halloween," Jessica said. "I was hoping you could take Clare trick-or-treating. Come for dinner?"

"Clare's not even three yet," Tommy said. "Is she ready to go trick-or-treating?"

"I'm just talking about taking her around the circle." Tommy and Jessica had purchased a McMansion on Hammet Circle right after they were married. "The neighbors would love to see her in her costume. You should, too. She's so cute."

"Well..." Tommy hesitated. Loud slurping let him know that Bull had finished his drink.

"C'mon, Tommy. Be a dad," Jessica cajoled.

"You're right," Tommy said. "It'll be fun. Will your mother be there?"

"Don't you start with me about Mom," Jessica warned.

"I know. I know. What time?"

"Come before it gets too dark—say before six," Jessica said. "And Tommy?"

"Yeah."

"This is good. Thank you," Jessica said and hung up.

"So, where were we?" Tommy turned his attention back to Bull. "Oh yeah. So a Mr. McCarter owns the place. Thirty acres. Did you find out anything special, unique?"

"Well, you saw that the house is up on a ridge," Bull said. "And I'm not sure, but there looks to be a creek at the bottom of the ravine, and maybe a waterfall."

"That'd be cool," Tommy said. "I'll have to figure out value." Tommy rose to leave. "Hey, Bull, couple things."

"What's that, Boss?"

"I looked at the maintenance file on South Towers."

"I can tell you about South Towers," Bull began to defend himself.

"Listen," Tommy said. "If it's important enough for Mike Smith to call me, we need to pay attention. I'm gonna need Smitty's help on a new project down below I-20."

"I get it," Bull said.

"Yeah. So go make nice with Mr. Brown and let's fix up South Towers. It's been a Kennedy Property since the 60's after all."

"You got it, Boss. What else?"

"Change out the thermostat to be computer-controlled... from my office."

"No problem," Bull said.

Tommy made his way back to his office via Rosemary's desk. "Call Mayme Shaw and get me a lunch appointment with her. And, oh, call Kellie for me and have her send JT and Caroline over on Wednesday afternoon. I want to see their Halloween get-ups."

Rosemary looked at Tommy, then set her jaw, "Some calls are better received when you make them yourself." She went back to the document on her computer.

Tommy stood there confused, open-mouthed.

Rosemary saved the document and stood up, all four feet, eleven inches of her. "Listen to me, Tommy Kennedy." She wagged her finger at him. "You think Mayme Shaw will take my call? Even on your behalf? It'll be more respectful if you call Mayme directly. I know Mayme and I know you need her on your side. You do as I say." Rosemary sat back down and began to proofread the document. Tommy headed back to his office.

Rosemary called after him, "And I'm not getting in the middle of you and your family."

Tommy closed his office door, grabbed a tumbler and poured himself a scotch.

Five

Wednesday, October 31: Early morning

Traffic around Lennox Square Mall was murder on weekday mornings. Tommy got to the Starbucks early to beat the crowd. He had an hour to savor his grande extra-bold Sumatran brew and enjoy the paper before his realtor, Kris Hansen, was due. The stereo played a Starbucks special CD offer of Richie Havens' "Here Comes the Sun."

Wednesday's edition of the sports section focused on high school football, and there was an article about the St. Laurence Knights. It mentioned JT as a team leader and major college prospect. Tommy got a little misty. He pulled the napkin from under his cup and held it to his nose, only a little higher on the bridge so that it reached the corners of his eyes.

After finishing the sports section, a metro section headline caught Tommy's attention: "East Metro Atlanta Housing Initiative to Face Important Vote." A picture of the Reverend Deacon and Alderman Johnson standing with Mayor White took up an eighth of the page. "And they're off," Tommy said to himself.

"Can I join you?" Kris was exactly on time.

"Good morning, Kris," Tommy said as he rose from his chair. "Can I get you some coffee and a danish?"

"No. No," Kris refused politely. "I'll get it. Be right back." Kris's big hair bounced and her spike heels clacked on the polished floor as she got in line. Tommy's eyes—as well as those of a few other patrons—followed the sway of her skirt.

After placing her double-skinny latte on the table, Kris reached into her folder, "I brought a copy of the market analysis of the Kennedy Lakes properties for you. We'd love to help you with that. What will we have to do to earn an exclusive marketing contract?"

Tommy took a long pull on his Sumatran roast and gazed across at Kris, "That's what I like about you."

"What?" Kris asked. She broke off a piece of banana nut bread and brought it to her mouth, pinky raised higher than her hand.

"You have the data, and you go for it," Tommy said.

"I'm good at what I do," Kris said, "and I know what I want."

"We'll get to that," Tommy promised. "What I want is for you to check out a property for me and give me a sense of value." Tommy then told her of the Camp Wahsega Road property.

Kris asked questions and took notes. "You know we have an office in Dahlonega. We'll have good information on that property," she said. "This is farther out than Kennedy Lakes. You expanding out there?"

"It's not for the company portfolio," Tommy said. "I want this one for me." He took another sip of his coffee. "Now, what kind of activity are we getting on Gaslight and Elmwood?" The Gaslight apartments were at an I-285 exit in southwest Atlanta, and Elmwood Plantation Apartments were out in Villa Rica.

"Gaslight is showing a lot of interest," Kris said. "It's in the pathway of development. Did you know about that?" She popped another bit of banana bread and then chased it with latte.

"I had an idea something was coming. That's why I think we can get a premium price for it," Tommy said. "If I can sell that and get rid of Elmwood, I can concentrate more in the Metro Atlanta area."

Tommy and Kris finished discussing real estate. "I think we'll get an offer soon on the Gaslight property," Kris predicted as she packed her folder and pulled a compact from her purse. "And I'll call you this afternoon with information on the Camp Wahsega Road property." They said their goodbyes before Tommy stepped into the restroom.

Heading up GA 400 on the way back to the office, the gleaming Basalt Black Porsche 911 Carrera sailed through the tollbooths with its Peach Pass. *I love these tollbooths. They're like barriers that keep the riff-raff out,* Tommy thought to himself. *What a great place to be—Roswell.* Then out loud, he said, "That reminds me. Maybe I should just stop in and see Ginny." The Porsche exited at Holcomb Bridge Road and headed to Councilwoman Virginia Wilcox's office in downtown Roswell.

"It's a great day in Roswell," the receptionist greeted Tommy as he entered.

"Tommy Kennedy to see Ms. Wilcox," Tommy told her.

Ginny heard Tommy at the receptionist's desk. She touched up her lipstick, plumped her hair and checked her teeth in her compact mirror. She then unfastened the second button of her blouse, revealing a little more cleavage. After a quick spritz of perfume, Ginny swept out, as smooth as warm honey.

"My, my, if it isn't Tommy Kennedy." She hugged him tightly. Tommy hesitated, but then returned the gesture. "To what do I owe this pleasure?"

"I was out and about," Tommy said, "and since we played so much phone tag these past couple of days, I thought I'd just drop in on you."

"Well, I'm so glad you did." Ginny deftly slid her hand around the rippled bicep hidden underneath Tommy's shirt-sleeve. "Come on back," she invited, winking at her receptionist as she led him to her office. "Get you some coffee?"

After sitting down at a meeting table in the corner of her office, Councilwoman Wilcox asked, "And what can I do for you, Tommy Kennedy?" She reached to fluff her hair around her ears and off her shoulders.

"There are a couple of things I'd like to discuss," Tommy started. Coffee was delivered as he began.

"Let me guess one of them," Ginny said. "That zoning change you requested for the RHS Condo project."

"That's one," Tommy said. "How's that coming along?"

"I think almost everyone on the Council is on board with that," Ginny said. "There's a point-of-information motion being raised by the Tax Watchdogs of Roswell."

"What do they want?" Tommy asked.

"Oh, don't worry about them," Ginny said, tapping a pencil on a notepad in front of her on the table. "They're just asking how much taxpayer money is being spent on the road reconfiguration you need that provides better access to the property."

"Do they know how much more tax revenue RHS Condo owners will pay once that old abandoned school property is repurposed?" Tommy's voice raised half an octave as he sat forward in his chair.

The beginning of a smile formed on Ginny's face, "Calm down now, Tommy." She leaned toward him and put her hand on top of his. Her blouse peeked opened perfectly. "I can handle those ole Watchdogs."

The vein receded back into Tommy's forehead. He settled in his chair and took a sip of coffee. "Thank you, Ginny. I know you can." His gaze lowered from the red gloss of her lips to where the lapels of her blouse met.

"You sound a little surprised, Mr. Kennedy," Ginny said. A raised eyebrow punctuated the comment.

"Oh, no. I'm not surprised at anything you can do, Ginny," Tommy said. "Hell, you were the only eighth-grader on the senior flag team in high school." He shifted to cross his leg and leaned heavily on an armrest, hands folded above his belt buckle.

"I'm flattered you remember that," Ginny said with a wink. She brought the eraser tip of the pencil to her lips. "Now, let me ask you a question."

"Fire away."

"You probably don't know, but I'm on the board of Birthright."

"Birthright? What's that?"

"A good Catholic boy and you don't know about Birthright?" Ginny admonished with a smile. "Birthright helps young women to consider alternatives to abortion."

"Oh yeah. Sure. Sure," Tommy said.

"Well, you see," Ginny continued, "we at Birthright are looking for new office space."

"Um-hmm." Tommy watched her as she re-crossed her legs to match him.

"Yes, and truly, it's a good problem to have," Ginny said. "Our services are becoming better known and more effective every day. And so...gosh, we need more space."

"I see," Tommy said.

"Well, Tommy Kennedy," Ginny said. "You have an empty office space in your complex."

"Yes, I do," Tommy said. "A couple of them."

"I know," Ginny said. "I was thinking..." She batted her eyes. "To be on Dogwood Road right off Holcomb Bridge, that would be a great location for Birthright."

"How about that," Tommy said. "How much rent can Birthright afford?" He took another sip of coffee.

"Well, you see," Ginny soldiered on, "Birthright has very limited resources. You'd be amazed at how far we stretch a dollar."

Tommy knew he was cornered. In his need for help with a zoning change, he had to play tit-for-tat with Ginny.

"I was hoping you could consider allowing Birthright a special lease rate," Ginny said. "It's such an important cause." She placed her hand on Tommy's arm.

"Yes, I'm sure it is," Tommy said. "So is my RHS project."

"That's right," Ginny said, sitting back in her chair, a twinkle in her eye. "I'm confident your zoning request will be granted."

"That's great, Ginny. I really appreciate it," Tommy said. "Let me check with my CFO, Ellen Krawshen, on our office space availability. She handles that for me."

"Thank you, Tommy," Ginny said. She leaned forward again and rested her hand on Tommy's thigh just above the knee. "We'd be ever so grateful."

A moment or two passed before Tommy snapped out of the mesmerized trance Ginny had lured him into and pushed his chair back to stand. Ginny caught him and said, "You mentioned you had a couple of things to talk about. Did we cover everything?"

"Oh yes. Of course," Tommy said, relaxing again in his seat. "Let me ask you—I know it's out of your district. Do you know Alderman and Deacon Johnson, and anything about the East Metro Atlanta Housing Initiative?"

"Well, I sure have read about the initiative," Ginny said. "Our council up here in Roswell is interested to see how they'll bring low-income ex-homeowners back into the market."

"That sounds so good, the way you say it," Tommy said. "Isn't that what the initiative is about?"

"I'm sure it is, but I'm not sure that's what Ms. Alderman Johnson cares about."

"What does she have to do with it?" Ginny asked.

"According to this morning's paper, she's put herself and her husband into the middle of it," Tommy said.

"So, what's that got to do with you?"

"This is still secret, but Kennedy Properties has a proposed development out that way. I thought we'd be a little further east, and so outside of Ms. Johnson's reach, but she's making inquiries."

"Aha! So you may need a little more of my help," Ginny bubbled with delight.

"Yes, Councilwoman. I may need a little more help."

They both stood and Ginny put her arm in Tommy's as she escorted him to the reception area. "I'm so happy you stopped in, Tommy," she said, hugging him again, too tightly.

"Thank you, Councilwoman Wilcox." Tommy took advantage this time and wrapped his arms around Ginny, his hands giving her a light pinch where her waist began its flair.

Wednesday, October 31: Mid-afternoon

"What prospects do we have for our empty office spaces?" Tommy asked Ellen when he finally got back to the office.

Ellen twitched at the sound of his voice. She pulled off her glasses and rubbed her eyes. "Huh? What'd you say?"

"Did I disturb your afternoon nap?"

"I'm sorry. It's just that Alex had a bad night. He's having seizures again." Ellen straightened in her chair and discreetly ran her fingers across her mouth and chin, checking for any drool. She then tugged her collar and smoothed the front of her blouse.

"Oh. Anyway, I asked about our available office space," Tommy said again.

Ellen rose to reach a file cabinet along the side wall. She flipped through a drawer, pulled a file, and sat back down. She opened it and returned her glasses to her face to read. "Looks like the usual sub-sandwich and smoothie suspects for the space next to the street."

"I don't want another restaurant gig in here if we can help it."

"Otherwise, it's been slow," Ellen said. "A few calls but no lookers."

"What would you think if we leased space to Birthright?" Tommy asked.

"I think that'd be fine," Ellen said. "They do good work."

"Yeah, but I'm a little nervous about how that would look," Tommy said.

"What do mean how it would look? Look to whom?"

"How would it look to our other tenants? To our clients and vendors? To the public." Tommy stared out the window behind Ellen.

"Birthright is not an abortion clinic," Ellen said, her hands folded gracefully on her lap. "You would never lease to one of those."

"Of course not," Tommy said. "But still, would leasing to Birthright be too controversial? Too churchy?"

Ellen's phone rang, showing an internal call. It was Rosemary. "Tell Tommy that Caroline is here. You should come see her—all decked out for tonight."

Tommy and Ellen walked out to the lobby area where his fourteen-year-old daughter waited. "Hi, Daddy. What do you think?" Caroline twirled to show the action of the tatters that hung off an Elvira-looking witch costume. Her face had the glow of a "look at me" freshman cheerleader.

Tommy stood back, but Ellen rushed over to get a hug. "You look so cute. And so grown up."

"Yes. A little too grown up," Tommy said with fatherly disapproval.

"Oh, Daddy," Caroline sighed.

Ellen and Rosemary gathered around her, and turned her this way and that to get all perspectives of a modern witch. Tommy could hear the chatter of tonight's plans for haunted houses and parties, but none of it registered.

"Doesn't she look the young woman?" Rosemary asked.

"Isn't that skirt a little short? And how low-cut should a fourteen-year-old's shirt be before it's past the cute stage?" Tommy complained.

"You're just being old-fashioned, Daddy," Caroline protested. She and Ellen sat on the lobby couch for more girl talk.

Tommy cringed as he watched Caroline tug at the skirt to make sure it covered everything. He could see way too far up her leg.

"Oh my God," he said. "You don't have on any panties. What—are you wearing a thong? Christ!"

Rosemary's objections to Tommy's blasphemous exclamations went unheeded. Tommy shook his head and clenched his eyes shut behind his hand, which rubbed his forehead. After a minute he asked, "Where's JT?"

"JT said he wasn't coming. He said that since you don't go to his games, he didn't need to come," Caroline said.

"He said that, huh?" Tommy winced. "How'd you get here, then?"

"Mom drove me."

"Where is she?"

"Out in the car, waiting."

Tommy flung the door open and left Caroline to talk on about her school and boys and cheerleading. He found Kellie parked in her BMW in front of the building. She unlocked the door and he got in.

"What in the hell is wrong with you?" Tommy demanded.

"Hello, Tommy. It's good to see you, too," Kellie said.

"What's with that outfit Caroline has on?"

"What? I think it's cute," Kellie said.

"Cute? It's slutty." Tommy was almost spitting as he registered his disgust.

"You're overreacting," Kellie said. "I was with her when she picked it out. It's an appropriate costume for Halloween."

"It's appropriate if she's gonna solicit on a corner," Tommy spewed. "Does she have on a thong?"

"You're being ridiculous. Everything is covered. Get over it," Kellie said.

"Get over it?" Veins were thumping on his neck and forehead. "That's my little girl. You should pay more attention."

Kellie stared, incredulous, at Tommy. "What did you say?" Her lips began to quiver. "Get out."

"Hu...what?" Tommy blustered. "You can't..."

"Get out of my car," Kellie shrieked. "You have a lot of nerve yelling at me to pay more attention. You don't even come to JT's games in his senior year, much less the JV games to watch Caroline cheer." Her voice began to crack, a tear formed in the corner of her eye. "Get out!"

So much static electricity had built up inside the car that Tommy's arm hair stood straight up. He opened his mouth— but then said nothing. He looked ahead at the windshield, but could not see out, as it had fogged over. He turned to Kellie, but still could not speak. His head was spinning, like he was strapped onto a spinning wheel in a circus act, the sharp-aimed knife-thrower artist getting ready to outline his spread-eagle body. To escape the daggers flying at him from Kellie's eyes, he opened the door and got out. He saw Kellie pull a tissue from her purse before he slammed the door and walked away.

Six

Wednesday, October 31: Late afternoon

Tommy lumbered up the stairs to his office. As soon as he opened the door, Caroline jumped up from her seat and hopped over to Tommy, giving him a peck on the cheek, "Gotta go, Daddy. See you Friday."

"Hey. Uh—bye." She was out the door and gone before Tommy could say anything.

"She's such a great kid," Rosemary commented. "So full of life and enthusiasm." Tommy mumbled something about short, revealing costumes on a little girl and headed back to his office.

"I'm going to head out early," Ellen said. "I've got to get Alex ready for tonight."

Tommy looked up from his desk and saw the wall clock ticks away from five o'clock. "Can Alex go trick-or-treating?"

"Oh, sure. That is, if his seizures don't attack," Ellen said. "But not like kids go door-to-door. His school has a party for them."

"That's great," Tommy said. "Hey, I've been thinking. I wasn't specific about the health insurance bids I want to see."

Ellen pushed her glasses up on her nose and then crossed her arms across her chest, "Oh?"

"I was reading about high-deductible plans."

A gasp escaped from Ellen a little louder than she would've liked.

"What's up with you?" Tommy asked.

"Huh?" As CFO, Ellen well understood the need for cost control, but how could she tell Tommy the impact on her and the collection clerks of his idea to pass on the premium cost of family coverage? And now he wanted to consider a high-deductible plan. "Nothing. I'll call our agent in the morning."

"Good." Tommy went back to the report he was analyzing.

Ellen pulled her glasses off her face and looked at Tommy. His finger traced a line across the page and his lips moved. After a moment, he realized he was being watched. "What?"

"What about you?" Ellen asked. "Aren't you taking Clare trick-or-treating?"

"Yeah. I'm going over there in a little while."

"You better get going," she said as she turned to leave his office. "Good night."

Tommy got up after Ellen left, and looked out over the office. No one was in the bull pit. Bull and Rosemary were gone. All the lights were on, but the place was empty.

"I swear these people have no respect," Tommy thundered. He went around flipping off light switches. He walked back to his office and poured himself a shot. He caught a glimpse of himself in the mirror and stared for a long while. Then he slammed back the drink and left the office.

The sun blinded Tommy as it pierced the windshield on his way to Hammet Circle. He punched in the code to open the gate to the community, and drove halfway around to his house.

"Daddy's home. Daddy's home," Clare screeched as she flew out the door and into his arms.

Tommy had to drop the flowers he brought so that he could catch her. "Look at my little Yellow Jacket."

"I'm a bumblebee," Clare corrected.

"Of course you are. You're the cutest bumblebee in the world." He scooped up the bouquet and carried Clare into the house.

Jessica leaned against the front door jamb, dressed in black leggings and a large, loose-fitting orange sweatshirt with a jack-o-lantern design. "Whataya got there?"

"These flowers seem to have attracted a bumblebee," Tommy said as he handed the bunch to Jess. She offered her cheek for a kiss.

"What's for dinner?" Tommy asked.

"Lasagna. My mother's here."

"Oh, great," he moaned as his cell phone gave its text message buzz. He pressed a button to check.

It was Bull: "I'm going to GiGi's up in Alpharetta tonight. Meet me if you can." GiGi's was a gentlemen's club. They were having a special show for Halloween.

"Who's that?" Jessica asked.

"It's Bull checking in. Your mom, huh?"

"Be nice," Jessica said. "She's excited for her granddaughter."

Tommy followed Jessica and Clare into the kitchen where Jess's mother, Kathryn, was putting the finishing touches on the dinner salad.

"Hello, Kathryn," Tommy said. "It's good to see you."

"Yes," Kathryn said, pulling a dressed piece of lettuce from the bowl for a taste. "It's good that you can be here tonight."

Tommy looked over at Jessica with a "that sounded okay" shrug.

"Jessica, everything is ready," Kathryn said. "Tommy, why don't you open some wine."

The bumblebee buzzed in and out of her chair, practically bouncing off the walls. "When are we gonna go, Daddy?" The stinger part of her costume bumped the floor as she fluttered from Jess's chair to Tommy's to Kathryn's, as if she were pollinating gardenias.

"Take a few more bites of dinner and we'll see," Jessica instructed.

Tommy's cell phone rang. "It's my realtor."

"You don't need to answer that now, do you?" Jessica said.

"Really important," Tommy said. "I'll be quick."

Kathryn snorted before taking a sip from her wine glass.

Tommy went into the living room for some quiet.

"This is Kris. You busy?"

"No, not really," Tommy said. "What'd you find out?"

"Well, 44 Camp Wahsega Road is an old homestead. Built in the 1940's," Kris rattled off. "One owner. No records of renovation or updates. What will drive the value is the waterfall at the back of the property."

"Waterfall. That's awesome," Tommy said. "Bull thought there might be one. What do you think?"

"Daddy. Daddy. Let's go," Clare yelled from the front door.

"There aren't any good comps," Kris said.

"There must be some indications," Tommy said. "Price per acre. Even square footage on the house. We can adjust for the waterfall."

Clare came into the living room and tugged on Tommy's sleeve, "C'mon, Daddy. Let's go twick-a-tweating."

"In a minute, baby. I'm almost done."

"Where are you?" asked Kris.

"I'm at my house. I'm taking my daughter trick-or-treating."

"Oh. That's nice," Kris said. "I thought you were separated."

"Price?" Tommy asked.

"Sure. Acreage out there can go for between $2500 and $4000 per," Kris said. "The amount of land was fuzzy, but I'd say the homestead sits on about thirty acres. And as beat up as that old house is—that's still probably worth $100,000. I'd say you're talking at least $220,000."

"Da-a-addy!"

Jessica came over from the dining room, folded her arms and stared.

"I gotta go," Tommy said. "Put together an offer at $220,000 and let's see what happens." He pressed "end."

"Really?" Jessica said.

"Twick-a-tweat. Twick-a-tweat," Clare chanted, bobbing up and down at the door.

"What? That didn't take long," Tommy said. He tried to unfold Jessica's arms to put them around him.

"None of that," Jess said. "Time to go." She had Tommy pick Clare up and pose for a picture before they left. The next-door neighbor kids were at the front door and the parade of witches and goblins and ghouls began, intermixed with princesses and action figures—and of course, a bumblebee.

Clare and Tommy were home in an hour. Tommy dumped a plastic pumpkin full of candy out onto the rug in front of the sofa in the family room. He lay down on his side, propped up on an elbow, as Clare sat across the pile from him. Jess flipped on the switch for the gas fireplace. She turned the knob for a low flame and then sat on one end of the sofa. Kathryn brought in the half-finished bottle of Chianti they'd been drinking.

"Mommy, look." Clare held out a mini Milky Way bar for Jessica to see. She then picked up a bag and brought it over to her, "Mommy, what is this?"

"It looks like," Jessica peeked inside the wax-paper bag, "a popcorn ball of sorts. Let me hold on to that."

Tommy was separating out all the Milk Duds and Reese's Peanut Butter Cups.

"Daddy, whatcha doin?" Clare asked him. She went around behind Tommy and crawled onto his back.

"Hey, my sweet. It's time you learned about the Daddy Tax," Tommy told her.

"Daddy Tax. I never heard that before," Jessica said.

"Mommy, Daddy's cheating," Clare complained. She climbed over Tommy and tried to pull the divided morsels that he'd culled back into the larger heap.

"Oh sure," Tommy said. "Daddy Tax gets imposed on Halloween candy and other goodies, like what Santa leaves in stockings and birthday cake—things like that."

Jessica burst, "Ha ha ha!" She slapped her thigh and grabbed her knee with interlocked fingers and rocked in her seat, her laughter dying down to a cute little snort.

Kathryn rolled her eyes, "Don't you cheat that child."

"No Daddy Tax," Clare wailed as she continued her efforts at incorporating the separate piles.

Tommy picked his favorites out and Clare would pull them back in. They went back and forth, round and round, and wound up throwing packs of Sweet Tarts and malted milk balls at each other with giggles and guffaws of fun. Jess got down on the floor with them, and the whole pile of candy was tossed into the air like so much confetti.

Kathryn sat stone-faced in the overstuffed corner chair. She cleared her throat and emptied her wine glass. Jess got the hint and put a stop to the bedlam, "It's time for bed, baby."

"I don't wanna go to bed," Clare moaned.

"Here. One more Tootsie Roll." Tommy poked around the mound of goodies and found a classic mini-log roll, unwrapped the piece, and tickled Clare's lips with it. She lurched to catch it in her mouth, but Tommy pulled it away. After a few more taunts, Tommy finally let her have it.

With a mouthful of chewy goo, Clare whined, "Do I have'ta goda bed now?"

"'Fraid so," Jessica said. "Tell Grandma good night."

"I'll take her," Tommy volunteered.

Clare toddled over to Kathryn and gave her a sticky good-night kiss. She turned to Tommy, "Tell me a story, Daddy. Goo'night Moon, Daddy."

"Okay, my sweet." He swept her off her feet with a flip and held her upside down for her to kiss Jess good-night. Jess watched with loving, soulful eyes as Tommy carted her off upstairs to bed.

"You better be careful," Kathryn said to Jess.

"Oh, hush," Jess told her mother. "Isn't this how it's supposed to be?"

"I don't want you to get hurt again," Kathryn said.

"I know, Momma. Me either." Jessica sat back on the sofa, took a long sip of wine and stared at the mess on the floor.

Tommy came back down after finally getting Clare to sleep. The room was back in its tidy shape. Smooth jazz drifted from the stereo. He started for the kitchen when Jess emerged carrying a newly opened bottle of wine.

"Where's Kathryn?" he asked her.

"She went home. Said to tell you goodbye." Jessica sat in her place on the sofa and put two empty glasses on the coffee table. "Want some?"

"Sure." Tommy sat next to Jess, sinking down in the plush sofa.

"Thank you for tonight," Jess said. She handed Tommy a glass of wine, and then poured some for herself.

"I had fun," Tommy said. He leaned forward, forearms on his knees. "I'm glad you called me."

"Me, too. I didn't want her daddy to miss out on her first real Halloween." Jess sipped her wine and looked away from Tommy, over at the fireplace.

Tommy sat back in the sofa, close, their shoulders touching. He leaned into Jess, his face in her hair, and drew in a deep breath, savoring her scent. Jess didn't pull away. After a few long moments, Tommy said, "I missed you Saturday night."

"Just Saturday night?" Jess asked.

"Well, no. I miss you a lot." He reached across Jess to put his glass down on the end table and moved in for a kiss.

Jess turned and offered her cheek, "I don't think I'm ready."

Tommy whispered in her ear, "Remember that weekend we stole away to the beach? We drank a bottle of velvety wine out on the deck, this same smooth jazz playing in the background, the sound of the waves." He put a hand behind her on the small of her back. His free hand ran across her stomach. He tried again for a kiss.

Jess kept her head turned as Tommy's nose nudged her hair away so he could get in a few nibbles on her neck. He brought his free hand back across her tummy. "Man, you taste good."

"Oo-o-oh. Now don't start that," Jess said.

Tommy worked those nibbles up to her earlobe and continued, "You were naked." Two fingers found their way under the waistband of Jess's leggings.

"Stop that. I had on a bikini."

He took a rose from the arrangement on the side table and stroked her cheek. "Mmmm," she let slip out as her head fell back onto the sofa cushion. Tommy then ran the rose from her forehead down her nose across her lips and over her chin. He flicked it from one side of her neck to the other.

"I feather dusted you that night, too. From your toes, to your thighs." The hand under Jess worked her sweatshirt up until it found skin. His free hand dropped the rose and pushed her hair back to cup her face and turn it to him as his mouth brushed her cheek on the way to her lips.

"Oo-o-u-um. No, really. Stop," Jess said, sitting up and removing Tommy's hands from her. "You know I want you. But not like this."

"Like what then?"

"I want to date again. Woo me."

"You know how much I love you. You know how sorry I am," Tommy said. He slumped into the sofa. "Can we ever get past that?"

"I think we can," Jess said. "But I need you to re-court me. You need to earn back my trust." She stood up and turned to him. Her thick, untamed black hair landed in waves over her shoulders.

Tommy looked her up and down. He knew the curves under the sweatshirt. "You are so beautiful."

"Thank you." Jess held a hand out to Tommy.

He took it, stood up, and embraced her. "How long?"

"I don't know," Jess said. "But please, let's date again. For Clare. For us."

The kiss good-night at the door turned into a prolonged *rencontre*. Tommy's hands again worked their way under Jessica's sweatshirt. "No-o-ah. You better go." She gave him a gentle push.

Tommy walked away with a slight hunch, looking at his feet, and wondered. How long could he hold out? How long would she make him wait? He was a man. He had needs. The Porsche's engine revved as he slipped it into gear. He left a little screech of rubber on the street in front of his house. He remembered Bull's message. *Maybe I'll head up to meet him,* he thought. Next thing he knew, he was at GiGi's.

The marquis on top of GiGi's building flashed hints of the entertainment inside: "Sabrina and Elvira have special treats for those with the right tricks" and other clever headlines. The parking lot was full, with a variety of cars ranging from Audi's to F150s. He found Bull's truck and a space nearby where he pulled in to park. He watched an older guy with a comb-over dressed in a trench coat enter the club. *Look at that old letch.* A carload of twentysomethings drove past him looking for a parking spot. *Is that what I look like to those kids?* Tommy worried. He backed out and drove away.

Seven

Friday, November 2: Mid-morning

"**I** would've come out to your office, you know," Kris Hansen said as she plopped her shoulder case on the chair next to Tommy. "It's my contract I need signed. You know the rules."

"This was easier. I have a lunch meeting downtown with the mayor, so it's on the way, more or less," Tommy said, rising to greet his real estate agent. "Get you a scone?"

"No thanks, but I'll have a coffee." The aroma of freshly ground roasted beans made it too hard to resist having a vanilla latte. Kris returned with her beverage, set it on the table, and removed her jacket. She leaned over to drape it on her chair, giving Tommy quite an eyeful.

"Did you hear anything yet on Camp Wahsega Road?" Tommy asked.

"I called the owner, Mr. Christopher McCarter, and asked if I could come out to see him. I told him I have a client interested in his property." Kris tried to sip some latte, but couldn't find the top of it in her cup, the froth was so thick. When she finally did, the surprise of scalding coffee caused her to jerk and hit the table, almost toppling Tommy's drink. "Sorry." A mustache of foam perched on her upper lip. Tommy reached across to wipe a spot she missed at the corner of her mouth.

"Anyway, Mr. McCarter said he wasn't interested in selling, but that I was welcome to come out," Kris continued. "Of course, that should be his first response. So I went over there yesterday."

"And?"

"And let me tell you, the place is a dump. McCarter is as nice as can be, but he has not kept up his place."

"Did you tell him my offer?" Tommy asked.

"Oh yeah, I told him," Kris said.

"You offered $220,000 as we discussed?"

"Of course. That's what you told me. That's what's on the contract."

"How'd he react?" Tommy asked. "Did he counter?"

"I'd say he didn't react at all," Kris said. "He just looked bemused."

"Did he ask any questions? Did he give any indication that he'd entertain any price?"

"Not really. He was the perfect gentleman. Very gracious." Kris pictured old Mr. McCarter coming out onto the porch in his cardigan sweater, leaning on a cane. "I told him you were a very motivated buyer, but he just wasn't interested."

"Hmmm." Tommy stared out of the window, deliberating over his next move. There were only a few suits traversing the sidewalks between the office buildings this late in the morning.

"Why would you want that place, anyway?" Kris asked.

"I just do. It reminds me of a place my granddad used to take me."

"As your realtor, I'm telling you, you made a very fair offer right off the bat. The house should be bulldozed. But even at $5000 per acre, and assuming a generous $100,000 for the house, $250,000 should be top dollar."

"Good then," Tommy said. "You go back to Mr. McCarter with that offer. Make sure he knows it's a cash offer."

Kris took her contract and lined through the dollar amount and wrote in the new number. "If that's what you want. Initial here."

"That's what I want," Tommy confirmed. "Go work your charms on the old man."

Tommy drove his Porsche across Lennox and down Piedmont to meet up with Councilman Mike Smith. Smitty had arranged a lunch meeting with Mayor White at the City Club to discuss, among other things, the East Metro Atlanta Housing Initiative. It was a tad early, but the noon crowd was already in evidence on the sidewalks. Waiting at a red light, Tommy enjoyed the sights and the talent walking by dressed in business skirts and leather jackets. *Hotlanta!* he thought as he pulled into a garage.

Tommy made it to the lobby of the building where the City Club of Atlanta occupied the top floor, offering breathtaking views of the city and surrounding countryside. He found the bank of elevators that went halfway up, at which point they required passengers to change carriages to go all the way to the club. The building did have an express elevator, but Tommy could see by its floor-level indicator that it would be a while before it arrived down in the lobby. So he got in an available car and began the relay to the top. Exiting at the City Club, he found Councilman Smith waiting in the foyer.

"Hey, Smitty."

"It's good you're a little early," Smitty greeted him. "Mayor White's office just called. He's on his way."

"Thanks for setting this up," Tommy said.

"No problem. Glad to help a friend and supporter," Smitty said. He replaced a journal he was reading on an elegant console adorned with inlaid wood. "Listen, are you prepared to give anything on this East Metro project?"

"What do you mean?"

"Did you see the article in the paper earlier this week?" Smitty asked.

"I saw it," Tommy said. "Great picture of Mayor White with Alderman and Reverend Johnson."

"I told you this was a hot potato," Smitty said in a hushed voice. "Mayor White can get a lot of good PR backing this initiative. You can help him with that."

Tommy was about to ask Smitty for his thoughts on how he could help when Hap Hampton emerged from the elevator. "Hey Tommy, Smitty. What are you boys doing here?" Hap's voice boomed through the lobby into the dining area.

"Just having a little lunch," Tommy said.

"Tommy, let's get together soon to talk about the east side. I think we can do good work together out there," Hap said with a slap on Tommy's back.

Mayor White walked in. A junior mayoral executive accompanied him. "Hello, Mayor, ole buddy," Hap bellowed.

"Gentlemen," Mayor White greeted them. Handshakes and back pats were passed around. "Good to see you all. Shall we?" Mayor White led the way into the dining area, followed by Tommy and Smitty. Hap stood in the lobby, eyes wide and mouth agape, watching the foursome in front of him.

Their table was in the corner of a semi-private section of the Executive Dining Room. Rich wood-paneled walls lined the room, providing a nice contrast to the bright, crisp tablecloths set with fine china and silver. A solo violinist played softly from a chair next to the fireplace. Airplanes took off from behind Turner Field to the south; the ridgeline of the foothills rippled to the northeast. And the view of concrete and glass buildings against the crystal blue Atlanta sky was magnificent.

"Mr. Mayor. Gentlemen." Maurice, Mayor White's regular waiter, greeted them. He was dressed in a starched white waistcoat and black bowtie. "Grey Goose with three olives," he nodded at Mayor White. "And for you gentlemen?"

"Boys, it's Friday. Let's have a relaxing lunch," Mayor White said.

After they ordered drinks and made the requisite small talk, Tommy commented, "What a nice article I read the other day about your hopes to revitalize some blighted areas south of town."

"Tommy, if we can be a catalyst to help the fine people of Atlanta find better jobs and better homes, well, isn't that what the mayor of Atlanta is supposed to do?"

"Well said, Mayor White," Smitty agreed with a nod. He brought his gin and tonic up for a sip.

Tommy asked the mayor, "You know of our Park Townes proposal? It sounds like it might fit well with your objectives."

"Oh? I heard from Councilman Smith here that Kennedy Properties may have something brewing in the southeast."

He popped the first of the olives in his mouth. "How far along are you?"

"All very preliminary at this point," Tommy said as he took a sip of scotch. "You may know, Mayor White, that Kennedy Properties has projects all over the west side of town, and up into the northern parts of Metro Atlanta. My grandfather started the company back in the 1940's, and those were the areas of town he grew up in." A busboy refilled water glasses and brought a basket of fresh bread.

Tommy continued, "Over the past few years, Kennedy Properties has been acquiring property below I-20, inside the Loop. And now with such low interest rates and what seems like a rebound in the real estate market, it may be time to move forward on our Park Townes development."

"Sounds wonderful, Tommy," Mayor White said. He spread a piece of bread with butter and took a bite.

"Yes, and so I wanted to visit a bit about the East Metro Atlanta Housing Initiative."

"What about it?" Mayor White asked, chasing the bread with a sip of martini.

Maurice appeared and with a slender silver bread scoop, swept away the crumbs from the linen tablecloth. "Your orders, gentlemen."

Over soup and salad, Tommy explained his vision for the mixed-use development he hoped to build. "There will be townhomes and single-family dwellings, with plenty of green space—a park with a pond, that sort of thing."

"And who is your target market?" Mayor White asked.

"That's the beauty of it," Tommy said. "I want to attract a range of people; singles and families, young and older. And pricing will be in the reach of modest income folks."

Smitty chimed in, "It sounds like Park Townes' income qualifications will be similar to that of South Towers. Is that right, Tommy?"

"Similar," Tommy agreed. "Yet, also more diverse. South Towers was my grandfather's first major development. He built it to help families with lower incomes have a decent place to live. Park Townes brings Kennedy Properties back closer to its roots."

"Excellent, Tommy," Mayor White said with real enthusiasm.

Four food runners hovered near their table. Maurice directed their placement. "Everything look right, gentlemen?"

"Everything looks fantastic," Mayor White complimented, and the servers vanished as quickly as they came.

"May I suggest wine, or refill your drinks?" Maurice was ever the professional. Fresh bread was brought, water glasses topped off, and the main course was underway.

"You know, Tommy, I wonder if the East Metro Initiative might be of support to your Park Townes," Mayor White said.

"Yes, I was hoping to talk with you about the East Metro Initiative," Tommy said.

"You know its goal is to help bring low-income ex-homeowners back into the market," the mayor said.

"That's what I've read," Tommy said through a mouthful of pecan-encrusted Red fish.

"Well, isn't that part of your target market?"

"It does sound that way," Tommy admitted. He sat forward, forearms braced on the table, utensils at the ready. "Alderman Johnson has sent a letter of inquiry on behalf of the Bedrock Foundation to Kennedy Properties. Frankly, I don't see the need to answer it. I don't understand how their foundation can add value to what we've been doing now for over sixty-five years. What I've heard from others is that Ms. Johnson can exact a pretty high 'pay-to-play or else' price on developments that are in areas she assumes are within her jurisdiction."

"Is that what you've heard?" Mayor White looked straight at Councilman Smith when he said it.

Smitty shrugged and carved off a slice of filet mignon.

"Well, I don't know about that," Mayor White continued. "The Reverend Deacon and Mrs. Johnson are fine people. They do good work for the folks on the south side of town."

"I'm sure they do," Tommy said. "And I mean no disrespect. But as I've said, Kennedy Properties has a long history of helping folks with comfortable, affordable housing. South Towers is our flagship."

"That's in my district," Smitty added. "I can attest to Kennedy Properties being a good corporate citizen." He followed that comment with a spear of asparagus and forkful of mashed potatoes on top of a bite of steak.

"I've heard some grumblings about South Towers through the grapevine," Mayor White said, finishing his last bite of salmon. He then drained his martini, and nodded to the busboy standing inconspicuously against the wall for another as he dabbed the corners of his mouth with his napkin.

"We're on top of that, Mayor White," Tommy said quickly. "I recently outlined to Smitty, Councilman Smith, our plans to update that property. It is so important to us that our tenants there feel secure and at home."

"In fact, Mayor White," Smitty added, "I was able to meet with the South Towers Tenant Association President just this week to review those improvements. They are very excited about it."

"Thank you, Mike," Tommy said. "Mayor White, I'm concerned that, at best, Alderman Johnson's involvement would cause our costs to increase. I'd have to consider bringing in a partner."

"And at worst?" Mayor White asked.

"At worst, we might have to table the project," Tommy sighed. "What would that mean to jobs and foregone tax revenues?"

"Um-hmm. And who might a partner be?" Mayor White probed.

"I know Hap Hampton has property in that area," Tommy said. "We've partnered with his company a couple of times on projects out west of town.

"Hap Hampton—that son-of-a..." Mayor White stopped short.

"I think it would be better to partner with Hap than to shoulder Alderman Johnson's add-on costs on my own," Tommy said. "Heck, I'd rather give you a ten-percent partnership interest than either of the other two alternatives."

Busboys began to clear the table as Maurice strolled up, "Coffee and dessert, gentlemen?"

"None for me," Mayor White said, patting the protrusion over his belt. The others shook their heads no. Mayor White leaned toward his deputy and whispered some instructions. Then he turned back to Tommy, "I'm glad we could get together today. Councilman Smith, thank you for arranging lunch."

"It was my pleasure, Mayor White," Smitty said.

"Men, please excuse us," Mayor White said. He and his associate got up from their chairs, as did Tommy and Mike. "Tommy, I'll be in touch with you soon."

"Thank you, Mayor White. Have a good weekend," Tommy said. Mayor White turned and strode out of the dining room.

"Smooth," Smitty said with a whistle.

Friday, November 2: Mid-afternoon

Feeling good about himself, Tommy decided he'd earned a reward—a drive into the mountains. He directed the Porsche out I-985 on his way to US 76, the Appalachian Highway. It was a bit too cold to take advantage of the convertible top, but still, it was a beautiful fall afternoon. There were plenty of tenacious leaves of red and orange clinging to their branches, though just as many of their faded brethren accumulated on the roadside.

Cruising west on the Appalachian Highway, Tommy thought of the masterful way he played Mayor White. He wondered how much of a check he'd have to write to Smitty's next campaign. The CD changer clicked and Tom Cochrane's "Life Is a Highway" blasted on the stereo. That brought thoughts of high school, which reminded him of Ginny Wilcox. He hoped she was right about his zoning change request for the RHS Condo project.

His cell phone rang, causing the music to fade. He pressed the Bluetooth button and answered, "Tommy Kennedy." It was Bull, calling with an update on his meeting with Mr. Brown out at South Towers. "Make it happen, Bull.

I just guaranteed Mayor White a major overhaul there, and Smitty stuck his neck out for me big time in our meeting."

At Ellijay, Tommy decided to turn south and cut back to Camp Wahsega Road. Driving one stretch of farm land between two mountains, he checked his speedometer—72 mph. He throttled back into the fifties. Rounding a tight curve, he saw the familiar split-rail fence. He thought about stopping, but then thought better of it, *Let Kris handle it.* He headed down to Dahlonega. What looked to be a hitchhiker wearing a plaid flannel shirt held a sign that read, "I Mean You." *Weirdo.*

He got back to the office about 6 p.m. A familiar sight— everybody gone, lights on, and too hot. He flipped switches and adjusted the thermostat before stopping in Ellen's office to leave a note:

"E –

Lights on and 82° at 6!

I need to review Park Townes organization docs on Monday.

T"

In his office, he remoted the TV to Fox News and poured himself a scotch. The computer came to life after a couple of minutes. He responded to emails, but there was nothing remarkable in them or on TV. He looked at his reflection on the back window for a moment, then pressed "J" on his cell to speed-dial Jessica.

"Hey, what're you doing for dinner?" he asked when she answered.

"Tonight?" Jess asked.

"Well, yeah. Tonight," Tommy said.

"You cannot call me at 6:30 for dinner tonight," Jess told him. "You didn't do that when we first dated. You can't do that now."

"Mommy, who is it?" Clare asked. "Is it Daddy?"

"And anyway, why aren't you at JT's game?"

"It's an away game."

"What? In Alpharetta?" Jess couldn't believe it.

"Yeah. Well, uh..."

"You're an ass."

"It's a meaningless game. They've already won the district."

After a cold void of silence, Tommy added, "Anyway, it's too late to get there now. How about Sunday afternoon? We'll go to a movie and then out to dinner—the three of us."

Jess looked down at two wide, eager green eyes looking up at her, "Okay. That'll be nice."

"Great. Pick you up at 3."

He surfed more news on the internet. After reading a few articles on the state of the economy, he clicked the Favorites button. He clicked through to the site *2 on 2*; it was not about pick-up basketball. A pop-up suggested that if the viewer liked what was displayed on this site, he might enjoy *Man 2 Man*. Tommy visited. A few scenes in, he decided to refill his tumbler. A few scenes more, and he had to visit the bathroom.

Eight

Monday, November 5: Morning

"**D**id you call Mayme Shaw to schedule a lunch meeting?" Tommy asked Rosemary.

"No, I did not," Rosemary said, chin jutting out. Her salt-and-pepper hair cascaded softly down her cheeks and into a loose ponytail.

"I thought I asked you to," Tommy said.

"And I told you that some calls are better received when made by you." Some of the rank-and-file employees came in the front door on their way to their cubicles.

"Godda…"

"Tut-tut," Rosemary held up her hand. "I'll have none of that kind of talk. You go back to your office, and I'll get your coffee." She looked at Tommy over the top of her wire-frame glasses, and he knew better than to rebut.

Tommy poked his head in Ellen's office, "I gotta couple of things to discuss. Come to my office as soon as you can."

Rosemary appeared after a few minutes, coffee mug in one hand, stack of mail in the other. "Please tell me you went to JT's game on Friday night."

Tommy took the cup from her, drew a sip, and looked at the mail pile.

"John Thomas Kennedy!" Rosemary scolded.

A slight flinch caused a splash of hot coffee to hit Tommy's upper lip.

"Good. Now, take a look at this." She picked up the top envelope and handed it to him. The return address showed it was from the United Way. "You need to pay attention to this one."

"But we already give to the United Way," Tommy said.

"Yes, but this letter is asking you to head up the Real Estate Division of next year's campaign," Rosemary explained. "We give a token amount to United Way now. This will allow all of us at Kennedy Properties to give back to the community in a more meaningful way."

"Oh my Go..."

"Tut-tut," she said with hand up. "You know better."

"But we already give," Tommy protested. "I don't have the time..."

Rosemary cut him off, "Listen, Tommy. I've been with Kennedy Properties all of my adult life. Your grandfather was a great man, and I promised him I'd look out for you, keep you on the right track. The United Way is on that right track."

"Yes, but my dad..."

"We're not talking about your dad. Did you know that Big John was on the board of United Way?"

"No."

"He was. It was very important to him to be a part of an organization that did so much good for the greater community. Giving money wasn't enough for him. He was actually on the steering committee that started fundraising this way—by getting companies to take a leadership position as an example to their peer competition."

"I didn't know that," Tommy said.

"Well then, now you do. You have an opportunity to step into some of Big John's shoes. You need to seriously consider saying 'yes' to them and putting Kennedy Properties front and center with the United Way." She folded her arms and looked intently at Tommy.

Tommy thought about what Rosemary said. He leaned back in his chair and stared blankly at the opposite wall. He brought the coffee mug up for a sip and remembered the few United Way luncheons he'd attended. All the players were there. And to have him and Kennedy Properties up on the video screen, getting recognition in front of the mayor and Mayme Shaw and everyone else...

"You're right, Rosemary. We'll do it."

Rosemary's unyielding eyes narrowed to a sharp pencil point. "That was too quick," she muttered to herself. She turned to leave when his cell phone rang.

"I made your offer as you directed on Friday," Kris Hansen said.

"And?"

"Mr. McCarter reminded me that he isn't interested in selling."

"Did you bring the offer out to him, or just call him?"

"I called him, but didn't get him till Saturday afternoon."

"I want you to go see him—meet with him."

"I did that last week."

"Do it again. You make a much more—ah—effective presentation in person." Tommy pressed "end."

Ellen appeared at his door in a frumpy cardigan and drab gray A-line skirt, legal pad in hand. Her hair was pulled back into a knot. A few wispy strands defied the styling and hung loosely down her cheeks. A pencil jutted out from its resting place on her ear.

Tommy waved her in and pointed to a chair. "Have you heard from our insurance agent?"

"They should have quotes for us later this week," Ellen informed him.

"Good. I want to see if we can save any money. Remind me how our 401k works. Do we have to contribute to that?"

Ellen gave him a quick summary of their Safe Harbor plan. Kennedy Properties contributed a flat two percent of everyone's pay so that Tommy could maximize the amount he put in for himself.

"You mean I put in two percent even if no one contributes for themselves?"

"That's the way the IRS rules read," Ellen said.

"How much is that?"

"That runs a little over $8000 per year," Ellen told him. "But remember, that allows you to put in about $30,000 for yourself."

"Yes." Tommy thought on that as he rubbed his chin. "Is there a way to tie contributions to how much an employee puts in? Sort of a 'help those who help themselves' approach?"

"You could do a Safe Harbor Match. That says that you'll match dollar-for-dollar up to three percent for those who contribute."

"And for those who don't?"

Ellen pushed those errant strands of hair behind her ears, "Nothing."

"And how many people actually contribute to the 401k?"

"I need to check," Ellen said, "but I think only four or five: you, me, Bull, Rosemary, and maybe the maintenance supervisors."

"So, if I match three percent for only those who contribute for themselves, how much would that save me?"

"I don't know offhand," Ellen said. "I'd have to pull the records and calculate it. But is that an expense you should worry about cutting?"

"Why not?" Tommy asked. "Every little bit helps. And besides, why should I contribute for someone who isn't saving their own money?"

Ellen thought for a moment, buying time by removing her glasses and rubbing her eyes, hoping to erase the circles underneath them. "You know how much the tenant relations people make. They probably can't afford to contribute. And geez, Tommy, even the measly two percent Kennedy Properties puts in for them is helpful to them, for their future. It's a good thing to do."

"Yeah, well, this is not a charity," Tommy said. "Let's see what a change to the matching program will do for profit margin."

"You're probably looking at two or three thousand dollars of savings at the most," Ellen said.

"Take that and add in savings from lower premiums from changing health insurance plans, and it all adds up," Tommy said.

"You're talking about people who hear sob stories all day long." Ellen stood up. "Who have to fight and push to get tenants to pay; who do all they can to increase revenues to Kennedy Properties. And for their reward, they'll bear more benefits cost and get less in their 401k. How can I deliver that message to them?"

"Good God, Ellen. Calm down," Tommy said. "Let's just see how the numbers shake out. I have a responsibility to run a cost-efficient ship." He picked up the phone and started to dial Mayme Shaw's number.

Ellen picked her pad up off the desk and stared at Tommy. She could barely afford to save on top of Alex's medical expenses. What would these changes mean to her and everyone else, especially those who were single parents like her? She left Tommy's desk glassy-eyed, went to her office and closed the door.

Tuesday, November 13: Noon

The home on Dunbar off W. Paces Ferry was as grand as its owner. Tommy drove the Porsche 911 Carrera around a circular drive bordered with Dogwood trees like spectators lining a parade route. Their autumn leaves had turned the luster of burnt maroon. In the middle of the swell of lawn, mature oaks towered from ponds of ivy kept neatly at bay by landscape professionals who maintained the stately manor's grounds. And of course, azaleas filled every available space under trees and around the house.

A manservant stood under the porte-cochere, waiting for the Porsche to come to a stop. "Good afternoon, Mr. Kennedy. Mrs. Shaw is expecting you. May I park your car?"

"By all means," Tommy said, taking off his driving gloves and handing the man his keys. Entering the mansion was like stepping back into antebellum times. A uniformed maid of African descent met him at the door to take his overcoat and direct him toward the great room. The heels of his Allen Edmonds clicked loudly on the polished marble floors. Tommy did his best to keep his mouth closed and contain himself at the grandeur of the foyer with its spiral staircase, crystal vases, and paintings by the masters.

Mayme Shaw, dressed in a flowing gown, shoulders wrapped in authentic rabbit, glided in from beyond the foyer to beckon him in. "Tommy Kennedy. I am so pleased you could come." Her voice was soft as silk. She held her hand for Tommy. He raised it to kiss it, and tucked it in his arm as she led him into the great room, which displayed even larger paintings and tapestries on the walls.

"This will be a small assembly," she informed him. "Mr. John Chalmers is here with Sister Marguerite from Catholic Charities. And I asked Archbishop Hardaway to join us. Come in. Come in."

"You are so gracious to include me, Mayme," Tommy said, slowing his gait. The other guests halted their conversation and turned to look at them.

Mayme, feeling Tommy's apprehension, stopped and turned, "It is time, my boy. It is time."

The fireplace crackled with well-seasoned wood as Mayme drew up to her guests, "May I present Tommy Kennedy." She introduced him to John Chalmers, CEO of Catholic Charities, dressed to the nines in a Tom James custom suit of navy wool in a herringbone pattern. Next was its executive director, Sr. Marguerite, who wore a smart business suit. "And you know Archbishop Hardaway."

"Yes, sir." Tommy stepped up to shake his hand. "Your Excellency. How good to see you again." He bowed and lifted the archbishop's hand to kiss his ring.

Archbishop Hardaway stepped in close as he withdrew his hand and placed it on Tommy's shoulder, "That's not necessary." Then, taking a step backward, he added, "I am so glad to meet you where we can visit in quiet. The Red Cross Gala was a little loud for me." Mayme and Tommy nodded in agreement.

The prim and proper manservant, the epitome of Southern gentility, carried in a bottle of 2007 Fisher Chardonnay wrapped in a linen cloth, offering to refresh everyone's glasses.

"Tommy, would you care for wine?" Mayme asked him. The man poured a dram into a glass, handed it to Tommy, and waited expectantly. Tommy lifted the glass to test the bouquet. He nodded and received a full pour.

Following behind the wine, the maid presented the guests with a silver tray of caviar on cucumber and other assorted succulents. Small talk centered on this year's Stewardship Appeal and the burgeoning Hispanic community. Sr. Marguerite mentioned the ever-persistent need for a home to better serve pregnant teens. They talked of the differing levels of support amongst the various parishes. Tommy stood on the periphery and nodded politely. His gaze turned to the large portrait of General Robert E. Lee on the far wall.

"Tell us about Kennedy Properties," John Chalmers requested. Tommy snapped back to attention.

"Why don't we move into the dining room, and carry on in there," Mayme suggested with a sweep of her arm, directing them through the foyer and into the dining room. In the dining room, mahogany wainscoting supported deep crimson walls. Silk cords tied back heavy drapery, allowing the day's sunlight to supplement the illumination of the wall sconces. Starched linen covered the table, and its leaves had been removed so that the five of them could sit in a more intimate gathering.

"Mayme, I declare," John Chalmers said, admiring the portraits hanging in the dining room. "Is that Mr. Shaw?"

"Actually, that is my great-grandfather," Mayme said. "He was born soon after the Civil War. He built this house back in the twenties." The crowd paid appropriate respect to her ancestry as mushroom soup was ladled into everyone's bowl. "Please, let's sit."

Mayme re-instigated the conversation, "Now, where were we? Oh yes. John, you asked about Kennedy Properties." She took a baguette and passed the basket as she explained, "Kennedy Properties was founded back in the late forties by my good friend John Kennedy, Tommy's grandfather. Big John and I were involved in many great works of charity beginning in the sixties. You remember... the civil rights issues and all."

"I've always wondered how you and Granddad became acquainted," Tommy said. The tinkling of spoons against china provided background noise, as did concertos and adagios playing softly on the home's sound system.

"Well, it started with his developing the South Towers," Mayme said.

"Is that a Kennedy Property?" John Chalmers asked.

"Yes, it is," Mayme continued. "Remember how it was back then. Big John wanted to have a nice property, but for lower-income folk." Mayme took a sip of wine and went on, "I, too, was very interested in better housing conditions for the poor. I became an advocate and a fan of Big John from then on."

"How marvelous," Archbishop Hardaway said. "So Kennedy Properties has a long history of fair housing practices. That will bode well for Catholic Charities."

"Thank you, Archbishop," Tommy said. "We have interests in a diverse range of properties."

Sr. Marguerite spoke up, "I wonder, with your expertise, Tommy, if you might help us with the Sister Gianna project?"

"And we're very interested in supporting the East Metro Atlanta Housing Initiative," John Chalmers added. "Are you familiar with that program?"

Tommy's head swiveled from the Archbishop, to the CEO, to Mayme, to Sr. Marguerite, and with widening eyes, back to Mayme. *How much is this lunch gonna cost me?* And the main course had not even been served yet.

Mayme sensed that Tommy might be feeling a bit overwhelmed. "Y'all can rest assured, Tommy will be honored to carry on in his grandfather's footsteps." Tommy felt the phone in his coat's breast pocket buzz and was thankful for the distraction. He began to reach for it, but Mayme reached across to place her hand on his forearm, and he thought better of it.

After lunch, Mayme held Tommy back in the foyer, her arm interlocked with his, while the others drove away. "You did well." She pulled him close for a peck on the cheek. "Don't worry about Chalmers or Sr. Marguerite. You'll be able to do a lot for them, but I'll pace them out."

"Thank you for that, Mayme," Tommy said. "But I don't know..."

"Don't you fret, now." Mayme patted his hand. "By the way, Mayor White called me last week to ask about you."

"Mayor White called about me?"

"Well, of course he did," Mayme's tone was as sugary as petit-four icing, eyes atwinkle. "He told me how well your lunch meeting went and he asked my opinion of you."

Tommy looked with anticipation at Mayme, like a little kid ogles wrapped Christmas presents. The mayor's help could be make-or-break with his east-side project. If Mayme put in a good word for him...

"Don't you worry too much about the East Metro Atlanta Housing Initiative," Mayme said.

Tuesday, November 13: Mid-afternoon

Tommy waited until he was on I-285 before checking his cell phone for messages. He pressed "send" to return Kris Hansen's call.

"Hey, Kris. Tell me something good."

"Tommy, you know me. I'm a straight shooter. I don't sugarcoat anything."

"No you don't, Sugar," Tommy said. "This doesn't sound like a precursor to good news."

"Let's get down to it," Kris said. "We got an offer on the Gaslight Apartments."

"That should be great," Tommy said.

"It's a low-ball offer. They're just testing the water."

"Well, what is it?"

"$5 million."

"$5 million!" Tommy sneered. A passing driver honked as the Porsche almost swerved into the next lane.

"I told you it's just a low-ball offer."

"The cash flow alone supports a $9 million value," Tommy said. "And that's not counting the locational value-add."

"I know that, and I told them as much," Kris said. "I really think they're just trying to see what you'll come down to."

"You know what?" Tommy said. "Let's not even respond. Who do they think they're dealing with? I'm Tommy Kennedy." He checked his blind spot and merged to exit onto GA 400.

"We'll do what you want, but I think you should counter," Kris advised. "You need to let them know that at least you're willing to negotiate to some degree."

"Yeah, yeah, I know the game," Tommy said. "How about let's counter at fifteen-and-a-half million dollars."

"Come on, Tommy," Kris said. "That's above your asking price."

"That'll show them how ridiculous they are."

"Will you trust me to handle it?" Kris asked.

"Yeah, alright. I know you'll take care of me," Tommy said. "What about Camp Wahsega?"

"You're not gonna like that either," Kris said.

"Just tell me what the old coot is saying."

"Remember, he doesn't want to sell."

"You go out there with the latest offer?"

"I called him, but Mr. McCarter doesn't want me to come out anymore."

"Does he realize I'm offering above market?" Tommy said. "What does he want?"

"He said he wants you to come out to see him," Kris said.

"Do what? What the hell for?" Tommy screamed. "Is my cash not good enough?" The Porsche slowed to 40 miles per hour, not a safe speed on the interstate. A GMC Yukon blew its horn as it threatened to rear-end Tommy's car. "Hey, watch where you're going," he yelled at the SUV. Then, back to Kris, "I don't have time for that. Who is this guy?"

"What else can I do?" Kris asked.

"Listen. Go back to Mr. McCarter with $300,000. Tell him that's my final offer—no bullshit. Cash and close in two weeks."

"Okay, if you say so," Kris said. "Why are you doing this?"

"Because I want the damn property. Now go get it!" He pressed "end" and threw the phone on the passenger seat.

Tommy floored it to get around an eighteen-wheeler entering the Holcomb Bridge Road exit ahead of him. The phone buzzed as he slammed on the brakes to avoid crashing into a soccer mom's van waiting at the light, causing the phone to fly onto the floorboard. Once stopped, he stretched to get the thing, "Yeah."

"Did I catch you at a bad time, my boy?"

"Oh. Hey, Brother Sean. No. It's okay."

"Tommy, I hate to bother you, and I don't want to push or anything, but time is creeping up on us fast," Br. Sean said.

"Huh?" Tommy said. "Oh, the Thanksgiving Community Dinner."

"Yes, my boy. I'm sorry, Tommy, but I really need you," Br. Sean said.

"I know. Alright. We'll do it," Tommy agreed.

"That's great, my boy!" Br. Sean said. "I knew I could count on you."

"I'll have Ellen cut a check this afternoon," Tommy said as he pulled into the Kennedy Square parking lot.

Nine

Thursday, November 15: Morning

"Shit. Damn. Shit." Tommy sat bolt upright in his bed, grabbed the alarm clock, shook it, and threw it across the bedroom. "Of all the days. Shit. Damn." A quick shower and shave, and Tommy was out the door in fifteen minutes. All that rush only to be stuck in traffic on GA 400 at 7:34 a.m. His cell phone rang.

"Mayor White here."

"Good morning, Mr. Mayor," Tommy said, putting on a practiced veneer of calm. "How can I help you this morning?"

"Tommy, I've got to get into a meeting first thing, so I'll get straight to it. I understand you have a meeting at Fulton County Courthouse."

"Ah...yes sir." Tommy wondered how he knew that. "I'm on my way there now."

"I presume it's about some tenant complaint," Mayor White said. "And court proceedings are public record..."

"Yes, but this is an arbitration meeting," Tommy said.

"Arbitration. Court suit. No matter, it'll become known," Mayor White said.

What will become known? And by whom? Tommy mulled.

"If you want my help with the East Metro Atlanta Housing Initiative and with Alderman Johnson's understanding of the value of the Park Townes development to her Bedrock Foundation, I need for you to eliminate any possibility of negative publicity."

"I understand," Tommy said.

"Good," Mayor White said. "I won't be associated with anything that could be construed in any way other than my being on the side of the people."

"Yes, sir."

"Fix it, Tommy. Quickly and quietly."

"I will. Don't worry." Tommy pulled a handkerchief from his back pocket and wiped his brow. "By the way, I've asked Ellen Krawshen, my CFO, to get with our lawyers and re-draft the organization documents on Park Townes to reflect a ten-percent ownership for you."

"Ten percent? I thought we agreed to fifteen percent."

"Er—uh—of course, fifteen percent."

"List it as the EAWIII, LLC, and send it to my office," Mayor White instructed. "I'll sign the papers as soon as I don't hear anything about your arbitration meeting today." Mayor White hung up.

Tommy exited I-75/85 to get over to Pryor Street and the Fulton County Government Center. He parked in a garage about a block away, behind the Mall at 82 Peachtree. A Salvation Army Santa stood next to a kettle in front of the mall and rang his bell. *Already?* Tommy kept his focus straight ahead. *It isn't even goddamn Thanksgiving yet.*

He met his lawyer in the lobby, "Remind me again what they want." *They* was the Associated Tenants Group, a membership of representatives from five separate Kennedy Properties' apartment buildings west of Turner Field, where the Braves play. Tommy reviewed the list of grievances and called Ellen.

"Remember, she went with Alex's class on their field trip up into the mountains," Rosemary told him. "A fall festival, apple-picking and all that. It sounds glorious."

"Goddamn, son-of-a..." The phone clicked. Tommy walked toward a wing of the building to get away from the pedestrian traffic. He re-dialed the office.

"I'll have none of that," Rosemary said when she picked up.

"You won't believe the morning I'm having," Tommy said.

"That's no excuse for taking the Lord's name in vain," Rosemary countered.

"I'm sorry," Tommy said. "Is Bull in there?"

"No. Bull is out at Kennedy Lakes this morning."

"That's right. Okay, I'll see you later."

Tommy called Ellen's cell, "Hey, Ellen, I know you're out today, but it's an emergency."

"As long as I can hear you over this uproar," Ellen said over the noise of the Riverside Academy school bus. Riverside Academy catered to special needs children like Alex.

"What do we have in the maintenance account? We're gonna have to take care of some things I've been putting off."

"Let me pull up the account," Ellen said. "If I disconnect you, I'll call you back."

After a few minutes, Tommy walked back to the lobby and interrupted his lawyer's texting. "Tell them we'll take care of everything on the list."

"Don't you want to argue this through? Come up with a compromise?" The young associate was only doing his job.

"No. Not this time," Tommy said. "Give them what they want. Don't go in front of the panel. Make this go away. Let Ellen Krawshen at my office know the outcome, and she'll get our property manager on it right away." He turned to exit the building.

The clang-clang-clang-clang of the Salvation Army bell accosted his ears. Tommy shoved his hands into his pockets and gave a wide berth to Santa as he headed to the garage. A panhandler approached him from the alleyway, "Buddy, can you spare some change?" His shirt was half tucked into pants that were two belt notches too big, and he reeked of cheap wine and urinal disinfectant.

Tommy kept his pace and made no eye contact, "Go away. Get a job."

Thursday, November 15: Mid-day

Thankfully, Rosemary was out to lunch when Tommy returned. A few cubicles produced a low hum of activity. Tommy made it back to his office unnoticed. He turned on his computer, then stepped into his bathroom while the electronics booted up. He washed the grime of downtown off his face. Returning to his desk, Tommy initiated a new message to Ellen:

"Do a quick revise of the Park Townes docs. List EAWIII, LLC as a 15% owner."

A swell of perfume broke into his chain of thought, "Oh, hey, Kris. I didn't know you were coming."

"I didn't either. But I was driving down from Alpharetta and thought I'd stop by."

"Not driving down from Dahlonega?"

"No reason for that," Kris said. "Remember, Mr. McCarter told me not to come out anymore."

"Yes. And when has that ever stopped you?" Tommy grinned. "Just kidding. What'd he say about my last offer?"

"He said he wants to see you."

"That old bastard." Tommy pushed away from his desk and swiveled around to look out the windows. What leaves were left on the trees had turned a matted version of their fall splendor.

"What are you going to do?" Kris asked.

"I don't know. What's going on with Gaslight?"

"Ball's in their court. I reviewed numbers with them and told them to come back with a serious offer that you could consider."

"Good. Good." Tommy got up to escort Kris to the reception area.

"Why don't you go see him?" Kris nudged.

"I don't want to talk about this anymore today. It's been a rough one. I'll think about it," Tommy said, putting it off for now. He watched her sashay out the door and down the steps.

On the way back to his office, a young female employee approached, "Mr. Kennedy, can I have a minute?"

Tommy didn't break stride or make eye contact. "What is it?"

"Mr. Kennedy, I feel I need to share some situations with you."

"Who are you?"

"I'm Denise Hawthorne." Denise had been at Kennedy Properties for two years; the first year as a part-timer while taking classes at the community college. Now, she was full-time.

"You're in tenant relations, aren't you?"

"Yes sir, and I want to share some of their stories with you."

Tommy stopped at his office door and turned to look at the young woman, "You report to Ellen Krawshen. You need to talk with her."

"Yes sir, I have. She sympathizes and even cries sometimes when I tell her about the harsh challenges of our tenants and their job situations, but she says there's nothing we can do. I thought maybe if you heard about them directly..."

"Ms. Hawthorne, your job is to collect the rents that the tenants have agreed by contract to pay."

"Yes sir. It's just that..."

"I'm not interested in feelings or excuses."

"I know, sir, but..."

"But, if you keep pushing to share your feelings and concerns, you'll find satisfaction in working third shift at McDonald's." Tommy closed his door while Denise Hawthorne remained standing in the hallway outside his office.

Tommy picked up his cell and pressed "J." He was about to hang up after the fifth ring when an out-of-breath Jess answered the phone, "Ha-hello."

"What in the world are you doing?" Tommy asked.

"I was out raking leaves, but I forgot to bring the phone outside," Jess said. "Thankfully, a few windows are open and I could hear it ringing." She took in a deep breath, held it, and exhaled slowly to reduce her heart rate.

"You always were a nut for the fall," Tommy said.

"I do love this time of year, with the change of color and the chilly evenings," Jess agreed. "Anyway, I'm glad you called. What's up?"

"Nothing much. It's been one of those days. I just wanted to hear your voice."

"Are you going to JT's game tomorrow?" Jess asked. "You know, Clare would love to see her big brother play."

"I wasn't planning to. It's an away game."

"Away? All the way down to Newnan? That's hardly away."

"Yeah, but if they win, they'll play at St. Laurence next week. Anyway, JT doesn't care if I'm there or not."

"I bet you're wrong about that."

"I didn't care if my old man was at my games."

"That's different, and you know it."

"Let's not get bogged down on this," Tommy said, dismissing the subject. "I was wondering what you're doing for Thanksgiving dinner. Have any plans yet?"

"Actually, yes," Jess said. "I thought we'd do something different, so I made reservations at that new Italian restaurant, Bocca. Want to join us?"

"By us, do you mean your mother, too?" Tommy asked.

"Yes, of course," Jess said. "I mean, my goodness, she lives here, and it's just us. You know that."

"Damn."

"What'd you think, Clare and me by ourselves?" Jess asked.

"I was just hoping it could be the three of us," Tommy said.

"Come with us," Jess said. "It'll be nice. And anyway, you know I'm not going to leave my mother alone on a holiday."

"I could leave your mother alone," Tommy said under his breath.

"Maybe it'd be better if you didn't come." And Jess hung up.

Ten

Wednesday, November 21: The day before Thanksgiving

Bull sat across the desk from Tommy, reviewing the progress on Kennedy Lakes and the list of demands from the Associated Tenants Group, when the intercom buzzed, "Mayme Shaw on line one." Bull stood to exit, but Tommy motioned for him to sit back down.

"Good morning, Mayme," Tommy said. "To what do I owe this pleasure?"

"Tommy, I just had to call you and tell you how wonderful you are," Mayme cooed.

"Wow. Thank you, Mayme. I don't get much of that."

"Well, you are," Mayme reaffirmed. "I was reading in this morning's paper about how Kennedy Properties was offering space to Birthright for free."

"You saw that, huh?" Tommy said.

"Yes, I did, and it's wonderful," Mayme gushed.

"You probably don't know, but an old friend of mine from high school is on their board," Tommy explained.

"Well, good for him," Mayme said.

"It's a woman," Tommy corrected.

"Good for her, and good for you," Mayme said, not to be deterred. "I know Archbishop Hardaway will be very pleased. This is exactly the kind of thing that reflects well on you, and therefore on Catholic Charities. Bravo."

"Thank you, Mayme."

"That's all for now. Happy Thanksgiving, Tommy."

"Same to you." Tommy hung up.

"I'm not used to you being so...bubbly on the phone," Bull said. "What's up with that?"

"Mayme Shaw saw the article in the paper about our giving office space to Birthright," Tommy explained.

"Did you say 'giving?'" Bull's eyes widened. "You mean you're not charging them rent?"

"That's right," Tommy said. "Ginny came through with the zoning change we needed on the RHS Condo project." Tommy paused, changing direction, "You know what? You should go out with her."

"With Ginny Wilcox?" Bull said. "That little flag girl from high school?"

"She isn't a little flag girl anymore," Tommy said. "In fact, I think she's attractive. Voluptuous."

Bull gave Tommy a sideways look, "Bullshit."

"No, really," Tommy said. "In fact, she looks kind of like this." Tommy reached down into his bottom drawer and pulled out a *Playboy* magazine. He opened it to the centerfold.

"You're full of shit," Bull said.

"Okay, she doesn't look like that," Tommy said. He flipped back to the section "Girls of the NAC." Tommy moved around to the other side of the desk to view the babes together with Bull. The magazine was open in full spread as they discussed the similarities of a particular dark-haired, full-bodied beauty from Carolina Tech to what they imagined Ginny Wilcox looked like when Rosemary buzzed on the intercom.

"Yes, Rosemary," Tommy said. He suppressed a smirk as Bull flicked at the coed's nipple.

"Mr. Steve Griffith is here to see you," Rosemary said.

"I don't know a Steve Griffith, and I don't have any appointments scheduled for today." Bull turned the page to find a red-haired beauty from University of Southern Appalachia.

"Mr. Griffith is with Workplace Chaplains of America," Rosemary said. "I think you should see him."

"I'm not interested in talking to any workplace chaplains. Tell him I'm busy," Tommy said.

"I've read about this group," Rosemary pushed. "You really should make time for him."

"Not interested." Tommy hung up. He resumed his pitch to Bull, "No, really, when I was in Ginny's office the other day, she had her blouse unbuttoned to here." Tommy pointed to the bottom of his sternum. "She looked good, I'm telling you." He turned the page back to Carolina Tech. "Yes sir. You should ask Ginny out." He held up the magazine for his and Bull's viewing pleasure when Rosemary walked in.

"Tommy Kennedy!"

Both Tommy and Bull nearly jumped out of their skin.

"Busted," Bull whispered out of the corner of his mouth.

Tommy slammed the *Playboy* shut. The centerfold page hung outside of it, but he crammed it back into the bottom drawer.

"So this is what you're too busy doing to meet with Chaplain Griffith," Rosemary said, arms folded and toes tapping.

Tommy's ears turned red. Bull shuffled around to the far side of the desk and looked down at his feet.

"Bull and I were reviewing progress on southwest Atlanta properties," Tommy said.

Bull took his cue, "Yeah. I'll get right on it, Boss," and he skedaddled from Tommy's office.

"I want you to talk with this man," Rosemary said.

"Really, Rosemary? We just gave office space to Birthright. I'm on the board at Catholic Charities. What do we need with a chaplain?"

"Obviously, you need more help." Her glare descended to the bottom drawer.

"As it turns out," Tommy said, "I do have a meeting, and I'm running late." Tommy grabbed his keys from the lap drawer and put on his jacket. He took Rosemary by the shoulders, turned her around and walked her out of his office.

Out in the lobby, Tommy greeted Mr. Griffith, "Please forgive me. I have an unexpected meeting to make." He motioned to the door and they walked out together.

"That's quite alright, Mr. Kennedy," Steve Griffith said. "I came unannounced."

"Yes, and I'm in a hurry," Tommy said.

"I understand," Mr. Griffith said. "Let me mention how we at Workplace Chaplains of America have a lot of success helping business owners transform their place of work into a Christian environment." The duo emerged from the stairwell and walked over to Tommy's car.

"That's great, Mr. Griffith. I don't think we need that."
Tommy pressed the unlock button, opened the driver's
door, and got in the Porsche.

"Wouldn't it be helpful, and more productive, if your
work force became advocates of Kennedy Properties in the
community because of your Christian leadership, instead
of clock-punching stiffs?" Chaplain Griffith stood just close
enough so that Tommy couldn't close his door.

Tommy turned the ignition and looked up at the chaplain, "Back the hell up, and go away."

Mr. Griffith's jaw fell open as he took a step back. Tommy
revved the Porsche's engine, slammed the door shut, and
sped off.

Wednesday, November 21: Afternoon

Most of the leaves were off the trees, opening clear vis-
tas to far mountain ridges that hadn't been visible a month
earlier when Tommy was first on Camp Wahsega Road. The
Porsche idled as he got out to open the gate. He could see
the winding of the tracks and how they switched back to
make it to the top of the ridge. Every few yards, there was
evidence of the trail having once been paved with stone and
gravel. But now, potholes marked the path up the mountainside and through the wood. Tommy eased the automobile
along, doing his best to avoid the pockmarks and preserve
the shiny, waxed Basalt Black finish of his Porsche 911
Carrera.

He pulled through a bank of trees and out into an opening in front of the old, worn-out homestead, which sat on
top of the ridge. There was no obvious driveway, no carport,

much less a garage. Weeds grew unchecked and choked what once might have been a lawn. They overtook any semblance of landscaping. The clapboard house hadn't seen new paint in decades. A strip of siding sagged below a windowsill. Only two shutters survived on all of the windows across the front of the house. One had at least a fourth of its slats missing. The other hung by only one screw as it leaned away from the window casing.

"What a godforsaken place this is," Tommy said to himself, as there was no evidence of life. He parked at an angle ten feet in front of the shack and turned off the motor. He got out and walked up the rickety steps, making sure to step on the riser's supports as he approached the rotting front porch. A screen door, minus its mesh, hung askew from rusty hinges. Tommy had to lift it to open it and move it out of the way. The front door sat tilted in its frame. One of the door panels had a fissure so large that he could see into the living room. He knocked lightly as he peeked inside. A sprinkling of paint particles fell on his eyelashes and nose, down to his shirt cuff. No answer. He knocked again and stepped back. Not a sound from inside the house, nor from out in the yard.

Tommy backed off the front porch and walked over to one side of the house. It sat so very near to the ridgeline that there was no way around to the back. "Anyone home?" he called. No answer.

Tommy walked around to the other side. Again, no access to the rear of the house because of the ledge. He stepped back onto the front porch and knocked again, harder. "Hello. Anybody here?" *I knew I should've called*, he thought. *How did Kris...* He jiggled the doorknob and discovered it broken.

It just rotated around and around, never catching, so that the door was not fastened shut. He pushed against the door. It was jammed in its frame. Peeking through the broken panel, he could see no one, no lights, nothing. Grabbing the handle, he pushed hard against the door, forcing it open. He stumbled in a half-step before he caught himself. "Hello! Mr. McCarter." The door creaked as he pushed it the rest of the way open and went inside.

The living room was in no better shape than the outside. Dust bunnies scampered across the floor. An old drop-leaf table with water rings from glasses left too long and strips of veneer missing served as a dining station and a catch-all for mail and whatever other odds and ends Mr. McCarter thought were important. A threadbare chair sat in a corner with a side table and lamp next to it. Musty residue floated in the stale air. Peeling paint dripped from the walls. Cobwebs and mice droppings were scattered throughout the room.

Straight across from the front door was an opening to the kitchen. A hallway to the left led to bedrooms. And in the middle of the living room's back wall, a simple wooden door must have led to...a backyard? Not with the house sitting on a ridge like this. Must be to a back porch. Tommy took a step in that door's direction when the familiar scent of antiseptic house cleaner in an odd mix with roasting meat simmering in a crock pot wafted into the room.

"Violet, I swear! You are a no-good good-for-nothing."

"But I scrubbed the bathroom top to bottom this morning."

"Don't you talk back to me," Johnny threatened as he slapped his wife.

"Daddy, why are you yelling at Mommy?"

"It's okay, Tommy," Violet said to her little boy as she cowered in the corner where the tub met the toilet. "Go outside and play."

"You stupid," Johnny yelled, lifting his hand for another slap. "He can't go outside by himself to play. He's too little." He turned to his son, "Hey you little mutt, go get me a beer." Johnny reached up to swipe the top of the medicine cabinet. With hardly a speck of dirt on his fingertip he yelled again, "Look at this filth. You can't even keep the bathroom clean." Violet raised her arms to cover her head as another onslaught came from Johnny.

"Stop it, Daddy," Tommy cried.

"It's okay, honey," Violet said. "It's Mommy's fault."

"Go on, you little mutt. Go get me a beer."

Tommy scurried down the hall to the kitchen. After he got a can of beer from the refrigerator, he stood in the opening to the living room, unsure what to do next. He was frozen there when his grandfather walked in.

"Big John!" Tommy shouted and ran to jump into Big John's arms for a bear hug.

"What are you doing with that can, son?" Big John asked. More yells and screams of anguish came from the hallway. "You go outside and play." He took the beer from little Tommy, put it on the table, and strode toward the hall.

"Where's my beer?" Johnny called as he came into the living room, coming face-to-face with Big John. Violet followed a few paces behind, sporting red finger marks on her cheeks and puffy eyes.

"What's going on here, son?" Big John asked, looking at Violet. "I taught you better than that."

"It's none of your concern," Johnny said. He popped the top and took a swig of beer.

Big John turned to Violet, "Go pack a bag for Tommy. I'm taking him for the weekend."

⸙

"Wheee, look at me," Tommy squealed as he raced his bicycle on the sidewalk in front of the house.

Johnny sat in his chair on the porch, wearing an unbuttoned short-sleeve shirt over an undershirt; beer can in one hand, *Popular Mechanics* in the other. Tommy rode by from the other direction, "Daddy. Daddy. Look at me."

After a big gulp of beer, Johnny looked out at his son, "What're you doing with those training wheels on your bike?" Tommy U-turned and whizzed by again. "Only sissies use training wheels," Johnny said. "Come over here and let's take those baby wheels off."

"No, Daddy. I can't ride a two-wheeler."

Stepping down from the porch, Johnny shouted, "Bring that bike over here, you little mutt. And go get me another beer." Tommy gave his dad a wide berth on his way inside as Johnny guzzled the last of his can of beer. He threw the empty on the driveway and crushed it with his boot.

Violet observed from the front door. She grabbed a beer from the fridge and went outside, little Tommy in tow, "What are you doing?"

"What's it look like I'm doing?" Johnny had found a wrench and was unfastening the bolts that held the training wheels to the rear axles of the bike. "No son of mine is gonna be called a sissy."

"He's no sissy," Violet said. "He's just too young for a two-wheeler."

"Shut up, woman." Johnny stood up and faked a slap. Violet flinched, hoisting an arm in a protective reflex. Johnny took the beer can out of her raised hand and popped the top.

"Please, Daddy. I can't." Little Tommy was on the verge of tears.

Johnny flipped the kickstand down, "Get over here, boy. Be a man and ride this thing."

"No, Daddy. Please." He wrapped himself in his mother's skirt, hoping he was hidden from view.

"He's scared, Johnny. Can't you see that?" Violet pleaded. "He's not ready to ride a two-wheeler." She put an arm around Tommy to hold him close.

"I said get over here, boy."

Shoulders drooped, Tommy shuffled over to the bicycle. He lifted a leg over the other side and placed that foot on the pedal.

"I'll give it a push and you pedal like hell, you hear me?"

White knuckles gripped the handlebar. A tear seeped out of one eye. A shove and then Tommy pushed down hard on the pedals and off he went.

"Pedal, boy. Pedal," Johnny yelled.

Violet stood there, paralyzed in her shoes, unable to speak or move. She made the sign of the cross and brought her hands into prayer position on top of her mouth to restrain a screech.

"Look up. Keep pedaling," Johnny commanded.

Tommy's determination was overcome by his lack of balance. He lost control and crashed on the sidewalk in front of the neighbor's house. The bicycle pinned his scraped knee to the cement as he pushed himself up on his hands. He started to cry.

"Oh, Tommy," Violet cried. She started to run after him.

"Don't you go to him, Vi," Johnny ordered. "He's got to man up."

"He's only five," Violet said and she went to go get him.

"I'll kick the shit out of you, woman," Johnny said. He took another swig of beer, then yelled out, "Get up, boy. You're okay."

Violet took two steps in Tommy's direction.

Johnny blocked her path. "I'm warning you, woman," he threatened again.

"Stop that crying and get up on that bike, you little sissy," Johnny yelled out at Tommy.

Big John pulled up in his Ford work truck and stepped down from the cab. "What in the world is going on here?"

"Just teaching the kid to ride a bicycle," Johnny said.

"Don't you think he's a bit young for that?" Big John asked.

Violet started bawling and went inside.

"Don't want nobody babying my kid."

"Baby a five-year-old? What's wrong with you?" Big John asked, exasperated. He walked over to Tommy and picked him up. "Hey, big boy. You're gonna be okay." He grabbed the bike and pulled it back in front of Tommy's house. "Go get in the truck. I'll be right back." He put Tommy down, patted him on the head, and nudged him toward the Ford.

He turned to Johnny, "I can't believe what I'm seeing. I never pushed you like that."

"I can't have my son being a sissy," Johnny said.

"You're wrong." Big John poked his head in the house and called to Violet, "Vi, pack a bag for Tommy. I'm taking him with me."

"What're you doing, Dad?" Johnny asked.

"I'm protecting my grandson."

"He don't need more protecting. Anyway, it's not your concern."

"You treat my grandson this way, and I make it my concern," Big John said.

Violet carried Tommy's backpack outside and handed it to Big John. He put it in the truck and drove away.

Tommy cried uncontrollably as the coffin that contained Big John's body was lowered into the grave. Violet pulled Tommy close, burying his face in her breast to console him.

"Stop that blubbering," Johnny ordered. He snatched Tommy away from the comfort of his mother. "You're acting like a sissy. It's embarrassing."

"Leave him alone," Violet said plaintively. "Can't he grieve for his grandfather?"

"Not at ten, he can't."

"Don't you have any feelings? That's your father."

"Well, crying won't do no good," Johnny said. "He ain't coming back from the dead."

"Don't you have any respect for the dead—for your father?" Violet started to cry.

"Woman, don't talk to me about respect for the dead. I saw plenty of that." Johnny spat on the ground to the side of the grave. "God rest his sorry dead soul."

"Oo-o-oh!" A vein throbbed on Violet's forehead, her ears turned red. She spun on her heel and walked away from the gravesite.

Tommy whimpered as he watched the grave workers shovel dirt on top of the coffin.

"Man up, boy," Johnny said.

Rosemary Bozeman, Big John's long-time assistant, walked up to pay her respects. She enveloped Tommy in her arms and he let loose again with sobs and sniffles.

"Now, there you go," Johnny said to her. "Look at what you did."

"You hush, Johnny Kennedy," Rosemary said. She rocked Tommy back and forth and hummed the hymn "What a Friend We Have in Jesus," which had the soothing effect Tommy needed.

"We'll have to get a notice out to the tenant associations tomorrow," Johnny said.

"I'm not coming in tomorrow," Rosemary said. "We—all of us in the office need some time off out of respect for Big John, and to gather ourselves."

"You don't come in tomorrow, you're fired," Johnny threatened.

"No I'm not, and I'm not coming in," Rosemary said. "No one is."

"Oh yeah? You need to understand who's in charge now," Johnny said.

Rosemary kissed Tommy on the top of his head, wiped the tears from his cheeks, and walked away. Violet and Rosemary crossed paths just out of earshot from where Johnny stood. He watched them embrace and then saw Rosemary holding Violet firmly by the shoulders, telling her something.

"What'd she say to you?" Johnny demanded when she joined them. "And anyway, where'd you go?"

"I was over talking with Father Anton. Tommy's going to become an altar boy."

"Altar boy," Johnny squawked. "That's for sissies."

"No it's not," Violet said. "You were an altar boy."

"Times were different then."

"Well, he's gonna do it."

"I'm not bringing him to church at 6 a.m.," Johnny said.

"You won't have to," Violet said. "I'll make sure he gets to Mass on time. It won't be a bother to you." She took Tommy by the hand and walked toward the car.

Johnny stood alone at the gravesite. "Sure, go be an altar boy with the rest of the sissies." He spat again.

Tommy finished tucking in his shirt and tied his shoes. The sun was not yet awake. He stood outside his parents' bedroom door. A harsh cough and hacking sound came from within. He knocked.

"Time to go, Mom," he called through the door.

"Honey, I'm not feeling well today." Violet endured another coughing spell. "Johnny, can you take Tommy to the church? He's got to serve Mass today."

"Ain't no way, woman," Johnny said. "I told you when you signed him up that I'd have no part in this."

Tommy knocked again and cracked the door open. More coughing and a spit into a Kleenex. Wadded-up tissues were strewn all over the floor next to his mother's bed, and a few were on top of the covers. He could see spots of red on them. "How am I supposed to get there?"

"I'm sorry, honey," Violet said. "I can hardly move this morning."

"You get out of bed, woman, or I'll tip the mattress over on you," Johnny said.

"I'll get myself there," Tommy said, and he closed the door. He heard another bout of coughing, hacking, and spitting come from the bedroom.

"Go on, sissy boy. Go help the priest," Johnny called after him.

Cleaning up in the sacristy after Mass, Fr. Anton picked up on Tommy's somber mood. "Tommy, you've been serving Mass for me now going on what...two years? I can tell something is bothering you. Tell me what's on your mind, son."

"It's nothing," Tommy said, putting away the chalice and flagon used at Mass.

"You're safe with me, son," Fr. Anton assured him. "Tell me what's wrong."

"It's my mother," Tommy said sadly. "She's not feeling good. I don't know what's wrong. She's never been sick."

"I bet she just has a flu bug," Fr. Anton said. "It's been going around."

"Yeah, I guess so," Tommy said. He took his alb off and hung it in the closet. He then slunk down in a chair and buried his face in his hands.

Sensing his despondency, Fr. Anton placed a hand on Tommy's shoulder. "You know, Tommy, you're my best altar server." The sacristy was dimly lit. The smell of incense lingered in the air.

"Thank you, Father," Tommy said through his palms.

"Always prompt and always knowing what to do," Fr. Anton continued. "And you're a big boy. How old are you?"

Sitting up, Tommy answered, "I'm twelve, Father."

"My. My. Only twelve and so big already," Fr. Anton said. Tommy just shrugged.

"You know what? It's time," Fr. Anton said with a hint of promise in his voice.

"Time for what?"

"It's time you earned your reward," Fr. Anton said mysteriously.

"Reward? What kind of reward?" Tommy's interest perked up.

"It's a special reward I reserve for my very best altar servers," Fr. Anton said. "It's a sacred reward, an honor and a privilege."

"I didn't know altar servers could earn a reward," Tommy became erect and alert in his chair.

"Like I said, it's very special and very private," Fr. Anton said. "It's secret. I think you're ready. Can you keep a secret?"

"Sure, Father."

Fr. Anton turned on the under-cabinet lighting and reached for something on a high shelf. "Come over here and take a look." He placed a magazine on the counter and opened it.

Tommy's pre-adolescent eyes bugged out at the picture of a nude woman. Tingles crept up the inside of his groin. "Father Anton, this has to be against the rules." Fr. Anton turned a page. "Wow!"

"I told you it was special," Fr. Anton said reverently.

"I'll say. I've never seen anything like that before."

Fr. Anton turned another page to display a different woman. "God sure does make beautiful things."

"Father Anton, this can't be allowed," Tommy said in a questioning tone, stepping back from the counter.

"Don't worry, Tommy," Fr. Anton said. "I wouldn't do anything against any rules, would I?"

"I...I guess..."

Fr. Anton turned another page and Tommy was lured back. "I can tell you like it." He noticed the bulge in Tommy's pants. He reached down and gave the protrusion a gentle pat.

"Hey!" Tommy jumped. "Uh...yeah. I'm not sure...Is this really okay, Father Anton?"

"Of course it's okay," Fr. Anton said. "I wouldn't reward you if it wasn't." He moved beside Tommy. "Turn a few more pages if you want." He put his arm around Tommy's shoulders.

A shaky hand turned a couple of pages and found another naked beauty. "Oh wow."

"Wow, indeed." Fr. Anton ran his hand down Tommy's back and around to his groin. Tommy was confused by the feelings he was experiencing. Sweat beads formed on his upper lip. Fr. Anton tugged at Tommy's belt and undid

Tommy wobbled out of the church in a haze. His legs felt very heavy. A couple of buddies called to him, "Hey, Tommy. Let's go play some touch football," but he didn't hear them or see them. His head was spinning. He wanted to be invisible. He wished he could go home. He just continued walking to the cafeteria to get some milk.

Blood-stained Kleenex and handkerchiefs were scattered around the bed and the floor. Violet lay listless, covered in sweat, and mumbling. Tommy knocked and peeked in his mother's room, "Mom, you okay?" The room smelled stale, like a dirty clothes hamper. A wet towel hung from a closet doorknob. "Mom, you better get up. Dad'll be home any minute."

Violet rolled over, face to the wall, and coughed. Tommy could tell it was weaker than earlier that morning. A car door slammed in the driveway. "Hurry, Mom. Dad's home."

"Why don't I smell any dinner? And where's my beer?" Johnny yelled from the front room.

"Dad, come quick," Tommy called from the hallway outside the master bedroom.

"What's going on?" Johnny demanded. "Violet, you lazy bitch. Get out of bed and get my dinner."

"Mom's really sick," Tommy said. "Maybe you should call an ambulance."

"Shut up, you little mutt," Johnny said as he pushed past Tommy and entered his bedroom. Violet's breathing was labored between a few meek coughs. She flopped onto her back and stared blankly at the ceiling, acknowledging neither Johnny nor Tommy.

"Dad, call an ambulance. Please."

"She'll be alright. Get me a beer."

The funeral director motioned for the pallbearers to wheel the coffin down the aisle. Johnny and Tommy followed behind and stepped to the side to watch as the coffin slid into the hearse. Tommy's shoulders heaved and his lips quivered.

"Don't you cry, boy," Johnny said sternly.

Tommy folded his arms tight across his belly as he rocked in his seat in the limousine. Tears streaked down his face. A low, muffled whimper escaped his mouth every few seconds.

"Stop it, boy. Time to man up."

"I'm sorry about your mother," Fr. Anton said a week later when Tommy returned to the server schedule.

Tommy moved zombie-like, reflexively performing the required duties of an altar boy. His face grimaced as he fought back tears.

"Come to me, son," Fr. Anton said in the sacristy after Mass. He engulfed Tommy in a hug and stepped back to help him take off his robe. He used a sleeve cuff to wipe the moisture from Tommy's eyes before he turned to hang the garment in its closet. "I know what will make you feel better." He reached to a higher shelf to pull down a different magazine. "You deserve something special after all you've gone through."

Tommy gaped at the depiction of two women naked together. "Do women do that?"

Fr. Anton turned a page, "Some do." Fr. Anton tugged at Tommy's belt. He slipped the boy's boxers to the floor, unsheathing the adolescent buggar. Tommy looked at Fr. Anton and then back to the picture. His young member throbbed.

Fr. Anton stood at Tommy's side with a small vial in his hand. Tommy saw him pour some of its oil on his hand. "What's that for, Father?"

"Here, let me."

Tommy forgot his troubles as Fr. Anton touched him.

Fr. Anton often gave rides home after school to his favorite boys. On an unseasonably warm day in October, he dropped Tommy off in front of his house. Johnny sat on the front porch in his wife-beater, which revealed his skull and rifle crossbones tattoo from his Army days, guzzling a beer.

"Who was that driving?"

"Father Anton."

"Yeah. You're gonna quit that altar boy stuff," Johnny said.

"Why?" Tommy demanded.

"Because it's for sissies," Johnny said. He took another swallow from his can. "Now that your mother's gone, you don't have to do that sissy stuff anymore."

"But I want to do it," Tommy said. "I like being an altar server."

"No boy of mine is gonna do sissy things."

Tommy stood tall on the threshold of the front door, "You can't make me stop." He ran to his room and tried to lock the door.

Busting through, Johnny yelled, "What'd you say, boy?" He flew at Tommy and shoved him up against the wall. Tommy tried to get away, but Johnny caught him, flung him back to the wall, and began chucking open-handed slaps to Tommy's face and ears and the top of his head. "You're gonna stop, or I'll beat the shit out of you."

Tommy sank to the floor under the barrage his father unleashed at him. "Stop!"

"Get up, you little mutt." Johnny kicked him on the side of the butt.

"One day, I'm gonna..." Tommy cried.

"One day you're gonna what?" Johnny unleashed another torrent, this time with fists.

Tommy shrank into a ball, trying to make himself as small as possible. He wanted to disappear. Who would help him now that Big John and his mother were gone? His dad was even taking Fr. Anton away from him. Who could he go to; how was he to get along now?

The next day at school, Brother Sean O'Flaherty stopped Tommy in the hallway of St. Laurence High School. "What happened to you, son?"

Tommy hunched down in his shirt collar, eyes cast downward and away, and mumbled, "Nothing."

"Who did that to you?" Br. Sean asked. "I don't remember any fights yesterday, or out in the fields this morning."

"I wasn't in a fight."

"Then what? Who?" Br. Sean pressed.

Tommy stared at his shoes.

"Did your father do that to you?"

"Can I go to class now?"

Later that afternoon, Br. Sean drove up to the Kennedy house in a restored Karmann Ghia. Johnny sat on the front porch, reading *Sports Illustrated*, a couple of crushed beer cans at his feet.

"Can I have a word, Mr. Kennedy?" Br. Sean called from the front of his parked car.

"No one's stopping you." Johnny didn't look up.

"I'm Brother Sean from St. Laurence High School. Let me first say that I'm sorry for your loss."

Tommy came to the front door to see who was talking.

"Go get me another beer, boy," Johnny demanded. Then, "What can I do for you, Mister...Brother Sean?"

"Tommy has quite a shiner," Br. Sean commented. He walked in measured paces toward the house.

"So?"

"Well, the funny thing is, there weren't any fights at school today," Br. Sean said. "Or yesterday."

"Yeah, so?" Johnny put the magazine down.

"I was wondering where he got that black eye."

"That's none of your business," Johnny said flatly. He stood up.

Br. Sean continued his steady approach to the house. "Do you know how he got it?"

"What are you asking?" Johnny crossed the porch to the top of the steps just as Tommy appeared in the doorway, beer can in hand. "If you're accusing me of hitting my kid, you need to mind your own business."

"My students and their well-being are my business, Mr. Kennedy." Br. Sean unbuttoned his shirt cuffs and began to roll up his sleeves.

"You better leave," Johnny said. He stepped down from the porch.

"Not until I get assurances that Tommy won't be abused."

"This is none of your concern."

"I'm making it my concern. I demand that Tommy not have any more black eyes," Br. Sean said. "In fact, he better not have a single hand laid on him."

"Alright, mister, since you want to stick your nose in it..." Johnny wound up to throw a punch. But before he knew it, he was jabbed twice in the face. Then an upper-cut to the gut doubled him over and he fell to the ground, gasping for air.

Tommy stood in the doorway and watched the whole affair. He saw his father fold in half and, as if in slow motion, timber backwards, splayed on the front lawn, a trickle of blood coming from his nose. He raised his eyes to meet the gaze of Br. Sean, who stood over Johnny, chest heaving. The beer can slipped from Tommy's fingers onto the threshold, sloshing its foam all over the porch as it rolled down from the door toward the steps. He inched his way back inside and closed the door. Backing away from the door, he hit the sideboard table and slid down into a squatting position on the floor, hands in fists holding his head at his temples, wondering, *What am I supposed to do?*

Out of the corner of his eye, Tommy noticed a brilliant gleaming around the door that led to the back porch, encircling it like a halo. The simple wooden door was transformed. Instead of a plain facade, it had become a dark, rich mahogany. Ornate carvings adorned the inside of each panel, and a stained lead-glass window graced its upper middle pane. The door handle was cast bronze with an intricate design of leaves and flowers surrounding a Celtic cross. Lights streaked insistently from behind and around the door, and through the perfectly cut stained glass. It sparkled and glittered, like lights that run around a movie marquis, only more amplified, more fluorescent.

The resplendent door beckoned to an awestruck Tommy. Magnetized, he drew closer, arm outstretched. With a tentative reach, his fingertips grazed the door, then recoiled as if expecting it to be hot. Hesitating, he again touched the majestic door, stroking it, feeling it. He studied the carvings of angels on the panels, caressing them carefully in wonderment. Overcome, he submitted to the door, leaning into it, pressing his face against the masterpiece, soaking its warmth into his skin. Finally, he clutched the knob, twisted, and pushed. And then he stepped through, out onto the back porch.

Eleven

S tepping onto the back porch was like travelling through a time-warp portal. The covered porch was in excellent condition—nothing at all like the rest of the house. The railing and spindles sported a freshly painted coat of bright white. Tongue-in-groove floorboards fit together perfectly and were stained a golden brown. In each corner of the porch sat different sized planters. Some were plain terra cotta, but others had Greek designs and muses stamped into glazed ceramic. The largest were filled with jasmine vines climbing up the posts, while bacopa and pink petunias trailed over their sides. Smaller ones tended vinca, dianthus, and geraniums. It was a riot of color, ignorant of the oncoming winter.

Along the back wall, raised-panel cabinetry housed a dorm-sized refrigerator. A microwave sat on a tiled countertop next to a sink. To the left of that, a couple of hand trowels and cutting shears rested on the counter. Empty starter pots and canisters of fertilizer sat on shelving above the counters. Three simple, slender vases graced the workspace with orchids, one with a white flower, the other two, different shades of pink.

The porch balanced on the very apex of the ridge. The view—which had been impossible to see from the front of the house—was spectacular. It looked across a valley that seemed to stretch for miles. A steeple rising from a distant church's belfry marked the beginning of the next mountain range's incline, which was dappled in reds and yellows against a brown that foretold the change of season. A falcon glided majestically on the updrafts, carrying the melodious chiming of the far-off carillon on its wings. The temperature was a splendid sixty-eight degrees. A wisp of crisp evergreen was in the breeze.

At the bottom of the property, a river ran from a pool where a magnificent waterfall cascaded, tumbling down the mountainside. Children's laughter could be heard floating up from the meadow on the other side of the stream.

"So this is why that old coot is holding out for more money," Tommy said, standing by the railing, gazing across the valley below.

"Hello, Tommy. I've been expecting you."

Startled, Tommy spun around to see an old gentleman sitting in one of the two rocking chairs on the porch. Thick white hair the coarseness of a cotton boll sprouted from his head. It was tamed back to spill over the collar of a button-down Oxford shirt. A maroon cardigan was buttoned at his midsection and covered the top of tan corduroys. A cane leaned on the wall against the counter near the door. "Won't you please sit?"

Tommy accepted the invitation, noticing intensity and also kindness in the old man's eyes. "How did you...never mind." Tommy turned his gaze back out across the valley. "That's quite a view you got there, Mr. McCarter."

"Call me Mac." He followed Tommy's gaze and inhaled deeply. "I love the smell of pine on a fall afternoon." After a few moments of quiet reflection, Mac asked, "How was your tour of the house?"

Tommy peered out another second, and then turned to Mac, "The hou...huh? Oh. This is amazing. This porch. The view. You got my last offer, didn't you?"

"We'll get to the offer in a bit," Mac said. "I'm so glad you came. I want to know a little about you." Mac took hold of his cup from the table between the chairs. "How rude of me. Can I get you some tea?" He stood easily enough, but paused at three-quarters of the way up to fully erect. Once Tommy got the full measure of Mac's broad shoulders and big hands, he could tell that Mac had probably been an athlete in his younger days.

"No, thank you," Tommy said. He watched Mac shuffle over to the counter and get a tea bag from a drawer and a bottle of spring water from the mini fridge.

Mac placed his full cup in the microwave and turned back to Tommy, "Tell me about yourself."

"There's nothing to know about me, Mr. McC—Mac," Tommy said. "I'm fortunate to have enough cash to offer you $300,000. What more do you need to know?"

"Sounds to me like you're quite the successful businessman," Mac commented. He removed his cup from the microwave and padded back to the rocking chair. "I suspect there are a few stories about how you came to be so successful."

"Just hard work and luck," Tommy said.

"I bet, but there must be more to it than that," Mac said. "What's that old saying? 'The harder I work, the luckier I get.'"

"Something like that," Tommy agreed.

"Would you say you're successful?" Mac asked. "Come on now, don't be bashful." Mac raised his cup for a sip of tea as he finished this last comment.

Tommy caught a gleam off the cup's rim. A wink, maybe? Must've been a reflection. "I've been called many things, but I've never been accused of being bashful," he said.

"Well then, tell me," Mac asked. "Are you successful?"

"You've got to be kidding," Tommy said. *What is it with this old man?*

"No, really." Mac drew the tea bag out of the cup with a spoon, wrapped the dangling string around them to squeeze out any excess, and then placed them on the saucer. "What does success mean to you?"

"Oh my Go..."

Mac held up a hand.

"...oodness," Tommy finished. "What kind of question is that?"

"A serious question," Mac said. "You want to buy this place. I want to know you better."

"Okay, old man," Tommy said. "I'll play along. My name is..."

Mac stopped him short, "I already know your resume. You graduated All State from St. Laurence, went on scholarship to Georgia Tech, own Kennedy Properties. I got all that." Mac leaned forward in his rocking chair. "I want to know you. What kind of man are you?"

Tommy sat back, crossed his legs, and began to rock. He looked out over the porch rail as he interlaced his fingers and raised them to support his chin. After a few moments of quiet, he took in a sharp breath and let out a sigh. "Okay, Mac. How do I tell you that?"

"Let's start with that first question," Mac said. "What is success to you?"

"Really, that's pretty easy," Tommy said. "I'd say success is having more money at the end of the year than at the beginning." His hands now rested easy on his lap.

"Is that it?" Mac asked.

"What more is there?" Tommy answered.

"All about money? That's pretty one-dimensional, don't you think?"

Tommy thought for a second, then expanded. "Well, that's the measurement in business—cash. And toys. In high school, it was winning the district championship and getting a scholarship. In college, it was winning the conference, going to a bowl game, and graduating."

"So, sports and profits," Mac reflected back to Tommy.

"Well...yeah," Tommy confirmed. "And net worth. What else is there?"

"If that's all there is to success, then you certainly have a bucket full," Mac said. "Let's see, car that gets attention, check. Boat in boathouse on Lake Lanier, check. Couple of McMansions and a beach house, check. Country club memberships, check. Armani suits and Toschi shoes, check. Jet off a couple of times a year to Pebble Beach and Doonbeg for golf weekends, check. Did I forget anything?"

Tommy just looked at Mac. *How does he know all this?*

135

"And now, a mountain house getaway, check." Mac traced the figure of a check mark in the air with his index finger.

"Let's cut to the chase," Tommy said. "Three hundred thousand dollars is more than what this place is worth, I figure."

"It's not about the money, Tommy," Mac said.

"What's this about, then? This definition of success thing?"

"What's missing from your definition of success?" Mac asked. He took a sip of tea.

Hmm, what's missing? Hell, nothing's missing. I'm successful. I can pay cash. "Let me think," Tommy stalled. His rocker swayed in slow motion as he stared out at the valley below. *What's this old coot want to hear?* He finally came up with something, "Hey, I'm on the board of Catholic Charities."

"Well, that's a move in the right direction," Mac said. "How's my friend Mayme Shaw?"

"She's...fine... How..." Tommy gave Mac a sideways glance. A wren fluttered from a hemlock's branch onto the railing, jerked its head to Mac, and then to Tommy, and then flew away.

"She's a good woman," Mac said. "She'll push you in ways that'll make you an asset to the community. After all, you mentioned net worth as a measure of success." Mac shifted in his chair and then asked, "Why did you give office space to Birthright?"

Tommy's jaw fell open as he stared at Mac.

"It seemed to have the desired impact you hoped for, yes?" Mac asked.

Tommy turned away and looked down at his shoes. He noticed a string of ants marching in a line under the railing.

Mac continued, "You see where I'm driving?"

"No. Not really."

"Intentions. Why did you give space to Birthright rent-free? Why are you on the board of Catholic Charities? Why did you accept the United Way's request to lead the Real Estate division?"

"Who are you?" Tommy demanded. "We've never met, so how do you know these things?"

"What? Do you think your actions are secret?" Mac asked. "You're Tommy Kennedy, after all."

Yeah. He's got that much right.

"Tell me, young man, why do you do the things you do?" Mac asked.

"Why does anyone do things?" Tommy answered.

"It boils down to intentions," Mac said. "Do you have altruistic intentions or selfish reasons for doing these things?"

"If I receive some benefit as a result of doing a good thing by helping out a friend for Birthright, or doing work for Catholic Charities, what's wrong with that?" Tommy asked.

"Depends." Mac clarified with a question, "Is it a genuine response of gratitude for the gifts you've been given or is it a business transaction, a quid pro quo?"

"Nobody has given me anything!" Tommy snapped. "I've earned everything I have. Yeah, I know I inherited Kennedy Properties, but I've grown the company. Saved it, really, from my father. Hell, when he..."

Mac gave Tommy a sharp eye, but Tommy rambled on, "...ran the company, it almost folded. He neglected the daily operations, ignored the basic business functions, never added a single property. All he ever did was drink beer on his front porch. If he hadn't died, who knows what would've happened to Kennedy Properties?"

"Who knows, indeed," Mac mused.

"Since I've taken over, I've gotten our financial house in order and built on what my grandfather started."

"And would Big John be proud of your business practices?" Mac asked.

Tommy jerked out of his chair and faced Mac, "Did you know Big John?" He stepped back a few paces toward the porch railing.

Mac rocked gently in his chair, hands folded on his lap. He smiled up at Tommy. A twinkle in Mac's shamrock green eyes communicated a warm acceptance rather than chastisement. Mac motioned for Tommy to sit again and said, "I've known Big John all of my life. I've known you since before you were born."

Tommy moved trance-like toward his chair, mouth agape at Mac. "What in the world? What are you talking about?" Though the temperature on the porch was a cool sixty-eight degrees, Tommy took off his jacket and hung it across the back of the rocker before he sat back down. "Oh God."

"Please, Tommy. That's disrespectful," Mac said. "You sure I can't get you some tea?"

"Yeah. Hmmm. Okay. That'd be nice," Tommy agreed without processing what was being asked of him. "But how about explaining how you know all these things, how you know Big John." Tommy twisted around to pull a handkerchief from the breast pocket of his jacket, wiped his face, then tucked it in his back pocket.

Mac paid no heed to Tommy's questions as he pushed himself up from his chair. In a few steps toward the counter, he was able to straighten. "Do you prefer lemon or honey?"

"Uh...honey, I think," Tommy said, his mind confounded from trying to figure out this Mac character. He could hear the clink of a cup, the opening of the mini fridge, the hum of the microwave. Mac's next topic brought him back in focus.

"Talk to me about how you decide to engage a new project."

"I've got a couple in the queue right now."

"I figured as much," Mac said as he brought Tommy his cup of tea on a saucer. On his way to retrieve his own freshened cup, he asked, "What analysis do you use to determine if one project or another moves forward?"

Shit. What is this, a real estate seminar? "Well, profit potential, of course," Tommy said. "That, and what resources we have and how best to allocate them."

"Resources? Like cash on hand, loan capacity, that sort of thing?" Mac clarified.

"That's it," Tommy agreed.

"Are the people you depend on thought of as resources, too?" Mac asked.

"I...uh...well, sure," Tommy said. "I assume—I mean, I've got to make sure we can manage a project from inception to operation."

"What do you think of the people—your employees, your subcontractors, inspectors and other government agency workers you have to work with? How do you treat them?" Mac asked.

"What do you mean, 'how do I treat them?' They have their jobs to do. I have mine," Tommy said.

"What kind of relationship do you have with these folks?" Mac asked.

"Relationship?" Tommy looked up off the right corner of the porch, searching his mind for how to answer. He doesn't think about the people or consider relationships. He knows he can't say that to Mac. "I'd say we have business relationships."

"How would you describe a business relationship?"

"I'd say it would be based on getting the best benefit possible," Tommy explained. "I'm out for what's best for me, and I assume others are out for themselves."

"A 'look out for number one' philosophy, if you will," Mac said before raising his cup for a sip of tea.

"I guess you could say that. There are people and companies that have skills and provide services I need. If the price is right, if it fits our profit model, then we hire them. They get paid. They make their profit."

"And if their price is too high, do you try to work with them? Find common ground?" Mac asked.

"Probably not. We just find another vendor who can fit with our model," Tommy said.

"Do you ever consider your vendors' ability to provide a decent livelihood for their employees?"

"Not my problem."

"Always the lowest bidder?"

"I'd say so. Yes."

"Useable and disposable," Mac challenged.

"Yeah..." Tommy caught himself. After a pause, he said, "I don't think I'd characterize it quite that way."

"Does a 'win-win' outcome ever fit into this scenario?" Mac asked.

"Like I said, we engage the people and the companies we need and they get paid—they win. We do so at a cost that allows us to make a profit—we win. We have to run our company efficiently. We have to make a profit."

"Is there more to business than profit?" Mac asked.

Tommy curled a finger into his tea cup and leaned back. He cradled the cup in both hands and brought it to his mouth for a sip. *Of course not. There's nothing more important than making a profit. But I suspect that's not the answer he's looking for.* "If we don't make a profit, we go out of business, Mac. It's just that simple. That's the way it is in business."

"Is any amount of profit acceptable?"

"What do you mean?" Tommy asked. "I don't think I could have too much profit."

"Sure," Mac said. "But for a small business, isn't profit somewhat fungible?"

"Huh? Certainly, profit is better than loss."

"I mean, can't you manipulate expenses to drive profit margin?"

"Prudent business practice demands that I manage expenses."

"What about the people who work at Kennedy Properties? Are they simply an expense, a profit or loss calculation? Or are they like family? Are they mothers and fathers? Sisters and brothers?" Mac asked.

Tommy looked over at Mac, opened his mouth to speak, but said nothing. *They're employees, for God's sake,* he wanted to say. He turned back to look out over the expanse. The sound of children's laughter drifted up from the meadow. Finally he said, "I've never really thought about it."

"Has Rosemary told you anything about how things were when Big John owned the company?" Mac asked.

The sound of his secretary's name caused a jolt to run up Tommy's spine. He turned again to Mac, slamming his tea cup down onto the side table, causing a splash of tea to slosh out over the rim. "How do you know Rosemary? She's never mentioned you to me. And believe me, she doesn't hold back on anything she thinks I need to know."

Mac's only reaction was to maintain his steady, easy rocking. Those shimmering green eyes in his genial face looked kindly at Tommy, easing his exasperation and somehow, redirecting his mind to the question at hand.

Finally, Tommy said, "I only remember how bad things were when my dad ran the company."

"Ah—Johnny Kennedy," Mac said.

"You knew my dad, too?"

"Of course I knew Johnny. He was a troubled man."

"He was an asshole." The speed of Tommy's rocking notched up a bit.

"I know how hard he was on you," Mac said. "How he belittled you and pushed too hard."

"Do you really?"

"Like that time when you were about seven and he made you stand at home plate while he threw fastballs at you," Mac said.

"Drunken bastard. He would chase me down and beat me if I moved." Tommy looked straight ahead.

"You were a scared and confused kid, rightfully so," Mac said. "And I don't mean to ignore the bruises he inflicted."

"And my mother never protected me from him."

"She was scared, too. It was a hard time for both of you." Mac's slow rocking came to a quiet halt. He asked in an even tone, "It's no excuse, but do you know about your father's service in the war?"

"Yes. Well...ah...not really. I always wondered," Tommy stumbled. "He had that tattoo."

"Johnny didn't like to talk about it," Mac said. "But you should know something of his experiences. Like the time he was part of a big offensive. He was on the very front line. In a foxhole for three days. Literally ten or fifteen yards from the enemy at times. Gunfire and grenade explosions all around. One night, a jet flew over and dropped a flash bomb, which lit up the entire field. Johnny looked up to see an enemy soldier in what looked like black pajamas on the verge of stabbing him with a bayonet. It was kill or be killed. That's a tough situation to live through. And there were many of those nights for young Johnny Kennedy."

Tommy tried to imagine the scene Mac had just described. He clenched his eyes shut and strained to get a picture of his dad in that foxhole. He couldn't do it.

"I think he lost his faith out there," Mac continued. "He never could transcend his experiences and forgive his enemies or his government. And Big John could never understand him. It was a chaotic time and a messy war. Still, like I said, that's no excuse for how he treated you."

Tommy turned away from Mac and pinched the bridge of his nose with his thumb and index finger. *The bastard.*

"Were there never any good times in your home?" Mac asked.

"None that I remember. Except when Big John would come get me." Big John would take Tommy for weekends, and sometimes for an entire week. Tommy would tag along when Big John made his rounds to apartment buildings he owned. They'd go fishing on Lake Lanier or on streams up in the mountains. And a couple of times each summer, they'd go see the Braves play. Big John would let Tommy have cotton candy, even if it ended up smeared all over his face.

"Big John was like a saint sent to rescue you," Mac broke in on Tommy's memories.

"Saint, huh? Yeah, I guess you could say that."

"Were there any other saints that came into your life?" Mac asked.

"Hmm...I don't know. I don't think of people that way," Tommy said slowly.

"What about Brother Sean?"

How does he know about Br. Sean? No sense in asking for an explanation. "Brother Sean is a great man," Tommy said reverently. "Say, did you play football?"

"Football? No," Mac said. "I did catch for a couple of different Mill League teams back in the day. Look at these knuckles." Mac displayed his gnarly hands, earned from years of catching fastballs in mitts with too little padding.

Tommy leaned back in his chair, "Everything I learned about being a man, I learned playing football for Brother Sean." Tommy's thoughts ran to the pre-game locker room speeches so rousing, he would've run full speed into a stadium's concrete support pylon with no helmet on if Br. Sean had told him to do so. He could hear Br. Sean pushing and cajoling him and his teammates to run one more sprint—that, when they'd already run fifteen after a two-hour practice. He was always pushing for one more: one more sprint, one more rep in the weight room, one more play on the practice field. Br. Sean taught them that they were capable of more than they thought possible. That with hard work and preparation, anything was achievable.

"Brother Sean has had quite an impact on the young men who've played ball at St. Laurence," Mac acknowledged. "He would never let any boy give less than his best."

"He made it such that you wanted to give your all," Tommy said. "He preached to us, 'As a man thinketh, so he is.' He made us believe that we outworked every other team, that we executed better technique, that we were champions and could not lose. You did not want to disappoint Brother Sean."

Mac added, "He'd demand one hundred and ten percent effort, rep after rep, until execution was perfect. What'd he used to say? 'It's not practice makes perfect. It's perfect practice makes perfect.'"

"I can hear him saying that right now," Tommy said. "I remember one practice session we were working on a double-team technique for our 44 power play. I'd block down on the tackle and when Bull got to him, I would slide off to the linebacker."

"That 44 power play is St. Laurence's signature play, isn't it?"

"Did you play for...no, you couldn't have. Anyway, it's a beautiful thing when properly executed," Tommy said. "But that particular practice, we just couldn't seem to get the timing right. Brother Sean had us do it over and over again."

"Must've been exhausting," Mac said.

"He got so frustrated that he got down in a three-point stance, nose-to-nose with me, screaming about technique. 'You gotta drive and release! Drive and release!'" Tommy sat forward in his chair, making hulking movements with his arms and chest, and imitated Br. Sean's deep coach's yell as best he could. "His face got so red, and in the middle of his rage, his tooth spat out."

"Tooth?" Mac asked, eyebrows raised.

"Yeah, Brother Sean has a false tooth, the one next to his front tooth. It flew out and landed right on top of my hand while I was in my stance."

"What happened next?" Mac asked.

"Everybody froze. We all just stared at the tooth and then at Brother Sean. And then I couldn't help it, but I started giggling. Well, that broke everybody up. We all just busted out laughing. Even Brother Sean. I handed him his tooth. He put it back in his mouth. We ran the play again and executed it to perfection. He clapped his hands and yelled out, 'That's what I'm talking about—perfect practice makes perfect.'" Tommy rocked easily, grinning at the scene playing out in his head as he looked out over the valley.

Mac slapped his knee and chortled at the story.

Tommy asked, "So, how do you know Brother Sean?"

"Oh, I know Brother Sean," Mac said. "I know he cares for you more than any other boy on any squad he ever coached. Look how he handled your dad."

"Hmmm." The ends of Tommy's mouth curled up slightly.

"And Father Anton."

Tommy leapt from his chair and wheeled around on Mac with a raised fist, "Don't... you..." Tommy spat and stammered. His muscles seized so tightly that it seemed his whole body shook with tremors. Mac and everything on the porch became a blur. Ringing in Tommy's ears drowned out all other sounds.

After what seemed like eons, Tommy dropped his fist and stormed off the porch, through the house, and out to his car. He slammed the Porsche into gear and spun two donuts around the front yard before gaining control and speeding down the path through the wood. The Porsche found every pothole in the atrocious dirt road, causing the tires to ram up in their wells and the Porsche itself to bottom out against the rocky ground.

Tommy finally had to stop before he'd find his beloved Porsche 911 Carrera in pieces down the hillside. He got out of his car and looked up and down Camp Wahsega Road. Slowly, he turned back to look up through the wood at the old homestead. He felt the cold November afternoon seep through his shirt. *Who in the hell is this guy? What in the world is going on?*

Tommy walked briskly up the trail toward the house. At the wood, he broke into a trot, and finally a sprint to the front porch and through the broken front door. Stopping in the living room to catch his breath, he saw again the streaming light emanating through and around the beautiful door that led to the back porch...and to Mac.

He strode over, threw open the door, and confronted the man, "I demand to know who the hell you are!" Tommy yelled, as intimidating in his six-foot-two frame as he ever stood, nostrils flared, eyes beaded, focused.

"You know me," Mac said in that same calm voice.

"What? That's crazy," Tommy spat out. "I don't know you."

Mac's soft eyes locked with Tommy's in a loving embrace that brought shivers to Tommy from his toes to his chest.

"I demand..." The scent of jasmine and the sound of birds chirping made Tommy aware of the warmth and beauty of the back porch. He dropped into his rocker. "How do you know about Father Anton?"

"It's okay, son." Mac reached over to lay his hand on Tommy's forearm.

A warmth passed through Tommy that penetrated deep in the marrow of his bones. "Please don't go there."

"It's time to heal those wounds."

"How can I ever..."

"First, know that what Father Anton did to you was despicable," Mac said. "Woe to the man who causes a youngster to fall, who is a stumbling block." Mac allowed a moment of silence by taking a sip of tea, giving Tommy time to calm down. Then he continued, "And thank goodness Brother Sean was there to intervene."

In his mind's eye, Tommy saw himself as the too-big-for-his-age seventh-grader sitting on the bench outside the locker-room showers. Br. Sean caught him watching the JV boys bathe after practice and called him to the office, "Shut the door, my boy."

"Yes sir, Brother Sean."

"What're you doing out there?"

"Just waiting to go home."

"You know I fixed it with your father. It's safe to go home. He won't hurt you anymore."

Tommy threw himself at Br. Sean in a big "thank-you" hug.

"There now, my boy," Br. Sean said, returning the hug.

Tommy unwrapped his arms, stood back a step, and began to unbuckle his belt and unzip his pants.

"What are you doing, Tommy. Stop that."

Tommy gave a puzzled look at Br. Sean, "This is what Father Anton has me do after Mass when we're alone in the sacristy. I thought..."

"No, son. We don't do that," Br. Sean said firmly. He paced in his office, grabbing an open can of warm Coke off the desk, and taking a long swallow.

Tommy was confused. A hot flash rose out of his collar and hovered over his face.

"Tell me, my boy. You say you serve Mass for Father Anton?" Br. Sean asked.

"Yes sir."

"He gives you rides home?"

"Sometimes."

Br. Sean turned to Tommy and held him by both shoulders, "Listen to me, son," he said, stooping to look straight into Tommy's eyes. "You are not to serve Mass anymore."

"But I'm on the schedule," Tommy protested.

"Don't worry about the schedule," Br. Sean said. "I'll take care of that and I'll talk to Father Anton." Br. Sean finished the Coke. "Does Father Anton touch you..." He pointed at Tommy's groin.

Tommy nodded.

Br. Sean crushed the Coke can and threw it across the office in the general direction of the wastebasket. The crumpled can ricocheted off the wall, bounced off the rim of the basket, and landed harmlessly on the floor. "Tommy, you know what Father Anton does with you...it's wrong."

"He says it isn't. I asked him if it was okay."

"Listen, my boy. I promise you, it is wrong. No one, nowhere, at any time should touch your genitals."

"But it feels..."

"But it's wrong. It's shameful."

"Father Anton said God made us..."

"Father Anton is wrong for what he's doing to you." Br. Sean grabbed Tommy on both biceps and squeezed hard. "You must believe me." He released Tommy and pointed for him to sit in a chair. "I'll deal with Father Anton." He paced some more.

"I don't want Father Anton to get in trouble," Tommy said, tears welling in his eyes.

"Don't you worry about that. You just stop serving at Mass. Come early to the gym if you want. No more rides in his car and absolutely no altar service. You hear me?"

"I guess so," Tommy mumbled.

"Look me in the eye," Br. Sean said. He pointed at Tommy's eyes with his index and middle fingers, then to his own eyes, then back to Tommy's and his own again. "Do you hear me?"

"Yes sir."

"You trust me?"

"Yes sir."

"Okay then. You got a ride home?"

Mac broke in on Tommy's thoughts, "What would you have done without that saint to intervene in your life?" He gave that consideration a moment to register. Then gently, he said, "No one knows about that time in your life, Tommy."

"I know about it," Tommy said quietly.

"Of course," Mac agreed quickly. "I'm sure you'll never forget it."

"It never quite goes away," Tommy admitted. "I'll go for weeks, and then my mind will wander into an old memory—dropping the soap in the showers, me holding some poor freshman while Bull snapped his bare butt with a wet towel. Then I'll remember the sacristy. I know I shouldn't dwell on it, but I like the memories. Then I catch myself."

"It was horrendous what Father Anton did. Diabolical," Mac said.

"And the porn." He turned his head away from Mac. "I'm so drawn to it. Even gay porn." Tommy's voice was barely a whisper. "Saying it out loud makes me nauseous."

A sudden bluster forced the few remaining leaves that clung tenaciously to the limbs of a Red Maple tree just down the slope from the house to let go. They swirled in a loose eddy, some rising higher than the roof and others drifting further down the ravine. Tommy followed one in particular as it floated its way onto the porch.

Tommy confessed, "I'm ashamed and embarrassed. I know it's wrong. And I'm not gay. Then why..."

"That is a very unfortunate effect of priestly abuse," Mac explained.

Tommy tilted his head and raised an eyebrow, thinking on Mac's comment. Then he said, "The smell of incense in church will bring on those memories."

"I bet."

"That's why I don't like going to Mass anymore," Tommy admitted.

"I can understand that," Mac said. "But staying away from Mass is not the answer. Listen, Tommy, I know you've been dealt a horrible hand. But it's your hand to play. You've got to figure out how to make it work, how to make a dead man's hand into a flush."

"I'd rather fold."

Quiet settled over the porch with the creaking of rocking chairs the only audible sound until a hawk screeched, soaring high above the meadow where children were playing. Tommy regarded the few buildings down below, clustered around a center court with a flagpole. The compound spilled out to an adjacent baseball field, a covered basketball court, and a soccer field carved out of the meadow that ran down to the river at the bottom of Mac's property.

"You have three beautiful children, Tommy," Mac said.

"Is there anything about me you don't know?" Tommy sighed.

"They're the biggest reasons why you can't fold," Mac continued. "But I'm afraid you're on the edge of doing just that with JT."

"You don't understand," Tommy said. "I remember how it was when I was in high school. I don't want to screw up JT like my dad did me."

"You're not going to screw up JT," Mac said. "His childhood was totally different than yours. You were a good father to him when he was growing up."

"Only because Kellie made me," Tommy said.

"Another saint in your life," Mac observed.

"Hmph. I'd get home beat from work, and she'd make me bathe the kids and put them to bed. Sometimes I'd be so tired that at story time, the book would fall on my face since I'd fall asleep reading to them."

"Maybe so, but they didn't mind," Mac said. "It was enough for JT and Caroline that you were there with them."

"Oh yeah? They'd shove and fuss to wake me up and finish the story," Tommy recalled. He reached for his cup on the table and drank the last of his tea. "Kellie signed them up for T-ball and dancing and Indian Princess and Cub Scouts. It was always something. She'd drag me to everything they did."

"She got you involved in their activities," Mac said. "She wanted your participation then, and she wants your involvement now. She's given her entire life to you and your family."

Tommy knew well Kellie's dedication to him. On the day the scholarship offer came from Georgia Tech, he and Kellie had been sitting on his front porch. "Yee-ow!" Tommy cheered, and he showed the letter to Kellie as he hopped out of his chair and danced his touchdown jig right there on the porch.

"That's awesome. I'm so proud of you," Kellie said. She got up to join in the dance. They romped arm in arm, her blonde ponytail bouncing in rhythm, making quite a ruckus in their celebration.

Johnny poked his head out the door to see what the commotion was all about. "What? No offer from Notre Dame?" is all he said, and he went back inside.

"Don't listen to him, Tommy," Kellie said, pulling Tommy into her arms. "Georgia Tech is perfect for us. I can go to Georgia State. We'll be right down the street from each other."

Tommy eased her away to look into her eyes—those robin-egg blue eyes. He kissed her deeply and held her tight, and whispered, "I love you."

"Kellie is your number-one fan," Mac said. "She always pulls for you; wants the best for you."

"I didn't always live up to her vision of my best," Tommy said. He recalled spring training of his sophomore year at Georgia Tech when he injured his knee. The coaches wanted to red-shirt him for the next season. Distraught, he sought the comfort of his high school sweetheart. He and Kellie had been dating going on four years by then, and the relationship had gotten very intimate. One particular encounter proved to be extremely close.

"When she turned up pregnant, I didn't know what to think. What were we gonna do? And then when she miscarried. I didn't even go see her for two weeks. It was during finals. I couldn't be bothered." Tommy's rocking stopped. He buried his face in his hands.

"You begged her forgiveness, and she readily gave it," Mac reminded him. "You married that summer. She was smitten with you. She loves you now."

"I don't deserve her love," Tommy said.

"Maybe not, but that's what love is," Mac said. "Think back to your young family life. Kellie made your home a refuge. You tried to stay in school. You played the next season at Georgia Tech, but then JT came along. You had to drop out, get a job, and make a go of it. After a couple of dead ends, your dad talked you into working at Kennedy Properties. She knew you loathed working for your dad. Still, she respected you for doing what it took to take care of your family."

Mac eased out of his chair and took the cups to brew some more tea. Tommy watched the kids playing on the fields below. When the buzzer let Mac know the water was warm, he added a few drops of honey to Tommy's cup. He then opened the fridge to get a slice of lemon. He pinched the wedge into his cup, returned to the rockers, and handed Tommy his cup.

"That's why she made your home a haven," Mac continued. "She knew that if you engaged with the kids, your family life would be infinitely better than what you had as a kid. She implored you to go to the mundane swim meets and tedious dance recitals. She begged you to go to Mass with them, to go to church as a family. She did all the right things to make your family one to be proud of. But she could never understand why you pulled away."

"I didn't want to screw it up," Tommy said. "I thought it was safer for my kids if I distanced myself from them. I didn't want to risk pushing too hard and lousing up their lives like my father did."

"Kellie figured that much out," Mac said. "She knew how harsh a man Johnny was."

"And unlike my mother," Tommy said, "Kellie is such a strong and wonderful mother to Caroline and JT. She's done an excellent job of raising them. But I could never go to Mass with them. I just couldn't go inside the church."

"She couldn't fight the demons she didn't know were in you," Mac told him gently.

"True enough," Tommy said into his palms.

Mac reached across to pat him on the back. "Still, she wants you in your kids' lives. And she wishes for your happiness with Jessica."

"How can she?"

"She signed the annulment without a fight," Mac said. "That's just how much she loves you—enough to let you go. So go to Jessica. It's a second chance. Not many people get a second chance."

"I don't deserve that...or her, either."

"No, probably not. But Jessica is like Kellie in many ways," Mac said.

"She kicked me out of the house," Tommy said.

"Well, okay. She stands up for herself more than Kellie. But she loves you the same way. She sees the man you could be, and expects you to live up to that."

"I'm tired of all these expectations," Tommy said, stiffening; his voice a half-octave higher. "Jess wants this. Rosemary wants that. Mayme expects this. Mayor White and Ginny play tit-for-tat. Brother Sean wants money. Everybody wants something from me." Church bells pealed in the distance across the valley.

"What do you want, Tommy?" Mac asked gently.

"I want it to stop."

Twelve

Wednesday, November 21: Late afternoon

Tommy lumbered over to the side rail of the porch and leaned out to look toward the front of the house. Same peeling paint and sagging boards he saw when he drove up. He noticed a cold wind on the back of his head and neck and immediately ducked inside the pristine surroundings of the porch. A spot on his temple itched. He scratched it as he walked over to the back rail and shook his head. "This place is unbelievable."

"I know you want it to stop," Mac said. "But the sacristy, the lingering memories, they will always be with you. It happened. It's not your fault."

Tommy turned around to face Mac. He folded his arms and gazed at Mac, trying to understand this strange and prescient man.

Mac continued, "Hiding behind the abuses of your father and Father Anton are keeping you from being the man you should be."

"Is that what you think?" Tommy said. "That I'm hiding?"

"I think that you use those experiences as an excuse, or rather as justification for how you handle business dealings and for reneging on your family obligations."

"What! I've never missed a payment to Kellie or to Jess," Tommy defended himself.

"Don't be so daft," Mac said. "I don't mean financial obligations. Come back and sit down."

Tommy ambled back to his rocking chair.

"Hear me, son," Mac went on. "You are called by God."

Tommy's face scrunched into a pug-like ball. He thought only priests or ministers of other religions were called by God. Being called by God made no sense to him outside the context of religious life. And his life was in no way religious.

"That's right," Mac went on. "Everyone has a God-given path to follow. And certainly, there are obstacles in that path. The challenge is to stay focused on God and not on the obstacles."

"Yeah. Yeah. Sure." Tommy's eyes glazed over.

"These are not just idle words, Tommy," Mac pressed. "Think about it. If you're honest with yourself, can't you see that God has endowed you with many gifts? And could it be possible that God is using the abuses you endured as obstacles to prepare you for something extraordinary?"

Tommy gave Mac another sideways "yeah, right" glare.

"That's right," Mac said. "You have exceeding talent. You're smart and you have a strong work ethic."

"You can thank Brother Sean for that," Tommy said.

"Undoubtedly, he fostered that in you. But you developed it, you've persevered," Mac said. "You can discern an unmet need and muster the drive to see things through. Your Park Townes project is an example of that."

Tommy looked out at the waterfall as he held his chin. He hadn't thought of real estate projects as anything other than ways to make money.

"And you're charismatic. Look at how people react to you, how they're drawn to you. It's a natural gift you have; an aura if you will. Why do you think Bull and Ellen stay with you?"

"Bull? Bull sticks around because it's easy to," Tommy said.

"Don't kid yourself. Bull could get a job with any construction or property management company. And Ellen? You don't think she could go anywhere and get better pay, not to mention better treatment? But she's devoted to you and to what Kennedy Properties could be. Why else would she put up with your cold-hearted scheming on cutting benefits?"

He knows about that, too? Tommy wondered. The mid-afternoon sun was just dipping below the porch's roofline, filling the space with a new brightness.

"And Rosemary," Mac expanded. "She sees Big John in you, and she's right. She has the highest hopes for you, and longs for you to lead Kennedy Properties like Big John did."

"How was that?" Tommy asked.

"To Big John, work was more than just a job, and Kennedy Properties was family to him," Mac said. "He measured success by how many people he influenced positively, for the good. He had a vision of helping people to have housing with dignity. That's why he developed South Towers. He cared more about what he gave than what he got. He felt an obligation to serve and give to the community. After all, it was the community that provided for his livelihood."

"Rosemary has mentioned something like that to me," Tommy admitted. "That must be why she keeps pushing things like the United Way and some chaplain group on me."

"I'd say so," Mac said. "You should pay closer heed to what Rosemary tells you." Mac raised his tea cup in a private salute to Ms. Bozeman, then carried on, "Big John loved his employees. He knew their spouses and kids; cared about their home lives. He believed that if he took care of them, they'd take care of business. He had that same attitude with everyone."

"The golden rule," Tommy said.

"Ah, so you do know something about 'do unto others as you would have them do to you,'" Mac chuckled.

"Twelve years of Catholic school didn't go entirely to waste." Tommy chuckled, too.

"That one maxim sets the best foundation for relationships," Mac said. He went on, "Big John appreciated the gifts he'd been given. He used his talents to the best of his ability, and he gave of his time and his money in gratitude and thanksgiving."

"So, that's what you were talking about earlier," Tommy said.

"You got a glimpse of that when you were with Big John as a little kid. Even at nine and ten years of age, you could grasp the essence of what is right and good, which is what Big John exposed you to. It's unfortunate that he wasn't able to reinforce those beliefs in your teenage and adult years."

"Boy, do I miss Big John," Tommy said.

"In high school, you participated enthusiastically at St. Laurence's Thanksgiving dinners for the community," Mac said. "You even cut the lawn for little ole Mrs. Snodgrass across the street from you and you wouldn't let her pay you."

"I remember her."

"Even during your first year of college, you were involved with the Fellowship of Christian Athletes. Where is that young man? Where is the Tommy who did good deeds out of the kindness of his heart?"

"He's grown up since then; gotten wise to the ways of the world," Tommy said.

"Baah! He's still in you; still a part of you," Mac disagreed. "But the muscles of kindness and compassion have atrophied from lack of use."

"Maybe so," Tommy murmured, his face shrouded by a vacant stare.

"Be the man that Big John would want you to be, that Brother Sean, Kellie, and Jessica want you to be."

"It's too late for me," Tommy said. "I'd be a hypocrite."

"P'shaw, it's never too late." Mac dismissed that comment with a wave of his hand. "The foundation is laid. However, getting back to that young and hopeful Tommy and growing from there is not easy."

"Ain't nothing been easy up to now," Tommy said.

"Maybe so," Mac said. "But this is a different kind of hard. And, you have to want it."

"I'm not afraid of hard work," Tommy said.

"That you can work long hours, I am well aware," Mac said, "but this goes much deeper than any physical challenges you've faced in the office or on the athletic field."

Tommy hooked the heel of his shoe on a cross-support bar of the rocking chair, and pushed on the floor with the other foot. He rested his head against the back of the chair and tried to imagine how his life would be better if he could make the changes in his life that Mac was suggesting. Could he be the adult version of the good kid he was in high school, or was that just a façade? He brought his tea cup to his mouth and rested the edge on his lower lip, but did not take a sip. He lowered the cup, placing it back on the table. "Maybe you're right. It'll be too hard. I don't think I can. Who would believe me, anyway?"

"Whoa! Quitting before you even begin?" Mac challenged.

"I am what I am," Tommy said. "Sure, I feel bad about Kellie and the kids. And Jess, too. But at work, it's eat or be eaten. If I start all this squishy caring and giving stuff, people will think I'm weak. They'll try to take advantage of me. I have an image to maintain."

"Oh, really?" Mac said. "How's that working for you?"

"Fine."

"Fine, huh? Is it fine how you have to fight all the time with tenant associations?" Mac threw at him.

"That's just part of the job."

"Is it fine how you have to compromise with politicians?" Mac demanded.

"Well...no. That's an aggravation," Tommy admitted.

"Is it fine how you drink yourself into a buzz every night because you can't go home to your wife?" Mac accused.

"What? Not every night."

"You enjoy maintaining the pretense of success that's defined by having the most gadgets and owning the finest gizmos? How silly."

"Okay," Tommy said, holding his hands up in surrender. "Uncle."

"Aren't those the very burdens of your definition of success you want to be rid of?"

"Yes."

"The demands and expectations of others that you want to stop?"

"Yes, I said."

"Is it fine how tense things are in your office?"

"Okay, I get it," Tommy said, turning toward Mac.

"Is it fine to be caught looking at porn?"

"That's enough." Tommy's answers became defensive, louder, more tense.

"Is it fine that JT won't return your texts or phone calls? Is it fine that your thoughts linger on shameful sex situations?"

"That's enough, I said." Tommy's face reddened.

"You said you wanted those thoughts to stop."

"I do. Enough already." He leaned toward Mac to emphasize the urgency of his plea.

"Do you really?" Mac asked.

"I said I do," Tommy shouted.

"I don't get a sense that you're serious."

"Come on, man. What do you want from me?" Tommy gripped the armrests of his rocker so hard that his knuckles turned white. The veins in his neck and forehead visibly pulsated.

"Which will it be, squeeze some maintenance expense money out of the Associated Tenants Group, or reconnect with JT?"

"Jesu..."

"Don't you dare," Mac stopped him. "Tell me, what's more important to you, Mayor White paving the way on your Park Townes project, or Clare growing up in a home with two loving parents?"

"Stop. Enough." Tears welled up in Tommy's eyes.

"How do you envision your future? Cuddling with Jess in your arms at night, or alone, cradling a tumbler, looking at internet porn?"

"Stop it." Tommy bent over, elbows on his knees, face buried in his hands. "Stop," he said in a muffled whisper. "I can't do it. I'm not worthy."

"No, you're not worthy," Mac said. He leaned forward to put his hand on Tommy's back, giving a little squeeze to his shoulder. "No one is worthy, son. Everyone falls short."

"What can I do? Tell me what to do." Tommy's hands slid around to grip fistfuls of hair.

Off the mountainside above the waterfall, another hawk emerged and spread its wings to catch the breeze. It glided down the mountainside and then up toward the porch, landing on a pine branch off to the left of the house. Its awesome beauty reflected the majesty of creation that lay before Tommy and Mac. After a few seconds, it leapt off its perch and swooped down to the creek below, banking further left and out of sight.

"Remember, I said it won't be easy," Mac said. "It'll take courage."

Tommy sniffed as he straightened in his chair.

"The first step is to accept that you are loved."

"Sure. I know that," Tommy said.

"No, really. I mean loved unconditionally. Despite the horrific things that happened to you, and no matter what you have done, God loves you," Mac explained. "You are loved because you are you, not because of what you drive or wear, or what you can buy, or even give—like making a donation or giving office space, as good as those things are to do. But loved just for who you are."

"God loves me. Great. But how do I really know?" Tommy questioned. "Who loves like... Oh, that's what you were saying about Jess and Kellie."

"And Brother Sean and Rosemary and Mayme," Mac listed. "And others."

"But I don't deserve..."

"It's not about what you deserve," Mac broke in. "They love you because you are Tommy Kennedy, deserving or not. That's one reason this is so hard."

"Huh?"

"You can't earn it. And you don't deserve it," Mac said. "But you are loved anyway."

Tommy certainly couldn't earn his father's love. No matter what he did, it was never good enough. *But Mac might be right about Jess and Brother Sean and the others.*

"Once you accept that fact and believe it," Mac continued, "you should feel safe to take the second step."

"Why do I need to feel safe?" Tommy asked.

"Because this is the really hard part," Mac warned. "And it involves taking a risk."

"What is it?" Tommy asked.

"You have to admit that you are broken."

"What do you mean, 'broken?'" Tommy asked, not liking the sound of it.

"I mean broken in the sense that you have faults and failings and weaknesses."

"Well, that's obvious with me, isn't it?"

"Obvious to me, yes," Mac said. "But as I said earlier, even as well as Kellie and Jess know you, they don't know what happened to you in middle school. And once you confess it, you'll become uneasy and restless. It'll make you vulnerable, exposed."

Tommy tried to wrap his mind around Mac's instruction. Could he admit his weaknesses? Out loud? To another person? To Jess? Maybe. To Bull? He shifted in his chair, stretching a leg out so that he could get his Swiss Army knife out of his pocket. He fiddled with it, flipped open a blade, then closed it; then he pulled out the screwdriver and tried to fit it in a slot on one of the rocking chair's arms, then he closed it. He then tugged at the scissors blade.

"See what I mean?" Mac said.

Tommy caught himself and grinned slyly at his fidgeting with the knife. He put it back in his pocket.

Mac carried on with his challenge, "That's why you have to be comfortable in the love of others, and believe absolutely that God's love is more powerful than any evil in your life. Because you'll worry that by admitting your shortcomings and your brokenness, you'll ruin your most important relationships."

"Right, because people expect me to be the strong, successful businessman," Tommy said.

"Exactly. But think about it, is that what the people closest to you expect?" Mac countered. "I mean, do you actually believe that Jessica married you because you drive a Porsche?"

"Well, she sure did love to go driving with me in the mountains with the top down," Tommy said. "But...no, not really. But Bull does. And James McKissick at the bank. And Hap Hampton."

"Honestly, do you care what Hap thinks?"

"No. But I don't want to confess my sins to him, either."

"That's a good point," Mac said. "It's not necessary to expose your weaknesses to just anybody and everybody. But, for those closest to you, it is absolutely necessary if you want a deep, close, intimate relationship. With those closest to you, you must be totally open and honest."

"I think I get it," Tommy said.

"And it's understandable that you harbor hate and anger towards your father. But who is harmed by that now?"

Tommy nodded. He knew well the rage that consumed him when he thought about his old man.

"So, what makes you a broken man?" Mac asked.

"My attraction to porn," Tommy mumbled.

Mac didn't hear Tommy and forged on, "One thing, maybe the biggest, is your mixed emotions of pleasure and shame over your memories of your altar server years. You are right to want to be rid of those thoughts. But it is the thorn in your side that won't be taken away. You must find a way to deal with them in a productive way."

"How can my memories of the sacristy be a good thing?"

"Those particular memories are not good," Mac said. "But it is because of your fondness for them that you must guard your thoughts. When you dwell on the desires of the flesh, you are like a rebellious child. Instead, turn your mind to the Spirit. In fact, say to yourself, 'come, Holy Spirit,' and see if you don't begin to experience a sense of peace. In that effort, you turn the source of your brokenness into the light of Christ, which can shine through you."

"Huh? How in the world would the light of Christ be in me?" Tommy said. "You know I don't even go to Mass anymore."

"And that separation from the sacraments and the Body of Christ is truly the shame of it all," Mac said.

"But how could I go to Mass with all that's happened, with all that I've done?" Tommy protested.

"No matter what happened, whatever bondage holds you, it does not disqualify you in God's eyes," Mac said. He sat up to unbutton his cardigan now that the afternoon sun streamed in. "He's not asking for perfection. He only wants you to try to submit to the Holy Spirit and learn His way of life. And when you fail, you need only repent humbly and try again. Anyway, you think you're the only man with transgression in his past? Moses killed a man. Peter denied Jesus—three times. Paul murdered Christians, for heaven's sake. Their failings didn't disqualify them; look at what they went on to do."

Mac sank back into his chair and continued, "Going to Mass is important. Mass is one of the best ways to encounter Christ. It provides an atmosphere where you should find it easier to let Christ into your life. And then you'll be better equipped to bring Christ to others."

"Bring Christ to others?" Tommy said. "That's not my responsibility."

"Tommy, son, let me give you an analogy," Mac said, rocking again gently in his chair. "You are like this old house."

Tommy's brow furrowed into a quizzical sidelong look. "You're off your rocker."

"I'm sitting in it right here." They both snickered before Mac explained, "No, really. Hear me out. What were your thoughts when you first saw the house, this old dilapidated ruin with a broken front door? 'Godforsaken' I think was the word you used to describe it."

Gee whiz, there he goes again! Can he read my thoughts?

"And from first appearances, you were right. The front of the house looks dreadful with its peeling paint, loose shutters, and battered siding. Yet, you were lured in."

"So, how does that describe me?" Tommy asked.

"Don't you see? You are the broken door. Even though you're in need of repair, you are functional, a door that can open and let folks in. And like the broken door, you need some fixing—a home improvement project, some putty to fill in the rotted-out spots, some sanding and planing around the edges. Thankfully, you have good wood below the imperfections, solid wood to work with. Brother Sean, Kellie, and Jessica all recognize that."

"I don't understand," Tommy said.

"When you got inside the house, what did you see?"

"Not much."

"Not much is right. The place is sparsely furnished. It certainly needs a good cleaning. It is paltry and lacking at best. That is, until you see the back door—that perfect, beautiful, magnificent, solid mahogany door. The incongruousness of that glorious door in that wanting space mysteriously drew you to it. You reached out for it, longed to touch it. And when you did, you lingered there."

"And so..."

"The majestic door inside the ramshackle house is like Jesus inside of a broken you. Even though broken and in need of repair, still, there resides within you the remarkable presence of Jesus."

"I still don't get it," Tommy said. "I mean, Jesus living in me? That's impossible. Frankly, it sounds kind of hokey."

"Remember what happened when you opened the door? You passed through it and discovered this sublime view from this wondrous porch."

"This is a breathtaking view," Tommy agreed.

"Exactly," Mac said. "So, here it is—letting people into your life so that they can find the Jesus in you leads them to this same spectacular view, metaphorically speaking. A view of Jesus in your life and in themselves. A sense of His love. That's what it's all about. Shouldn't you want everyone in your life, even everyone you meet, to have the opportunity to encounter this?" Mac waved his hand like waving a wand over his kingdom. A rainbow formed on the mist rising from the waterfall.

The rainbow's vivid red, orange, yellow, green, blue, indigo, and violet colors were distinct, yet blended in a spectral smearing in their arc. Tommy arose from his chair and went to the railing to reach out to try to touch it. So captivated was he by the iridescence that he opened the side gate and stepped down off the porch. A pathway meandered through mountain laurel, hardwoods, and evergreens. November's cool air kept the musty smell of decaying leaves and pine needles close to Tommy as they cushioned the trail, traversing a series of switchbacks on its way to the river. The rainbow remained directly above his head, just beyond his reach.

At the bottom of the ravine, he became aware again of the children's laughter. Tommy hopscotched across the river on some boulders and landed on the edge of the soccer field. The children stopped their game and ran to Tommy in defiance of the whistles and shouts of their counselors. The first to him crashed into his body in an unreserved hug. The others arrived within seconds and encircled Tommy, tugging him along, beckoning him to the field. He was laughing. The children were laughing. A feeling of joy overwhelmed him.

Once the counselors regained control and engaged the kids in their game, Tommy noticed that these were no ordinary children. They had a glow about them, an aura. That's when it struck him. Some of the kids' eyes bulged a little. Some ran with gimps, if they could run at all. Some would get to the soccer ball and kick, and completely miss, all to uproarious hilarity. Some milled about in groups of two or three and watched and cheered. They all played with abandon and bliss.

Tommy had never seen such happiness and enthusiasm before. He couldn't help himself; he joined in the game, kicking the ball back and forth with a cloud of children surrounding him, orbiting around him as they drifted up and down the field.

After a while, whistles blew and counselors called an end to the game. Tommy watched them bound and skip and make their way up the field toward the flagpole and the buildings beyond. It dawned on him that one of those kids could be Alex. He thought of Ellen Krawshen. As exhausted as she seemed at times, she must have occasions for intense joy like this as well. He realized he knew nothing of Ellen's life outside the office. He knew nothing of Rosemary's life. He didn't even know everybody's name.

He rushed back up the slope to Mac's porch. "That was incredible! Is that what you're talking about?"

Mac looked up at Tommy and grinned, "You just caught a glimpse, an inkling of the peace and joy you could have in your life if you choose to."

"How do I do that?" Tommy wondered. "It's taken thirty-eight years for me to become who I am. I can't change overnight...can I?"

"You tell me," Mac said. He sipped his tea. As he gazed out, the rainbow faded from view. "But for the want of a little courage, the whole world could be transformed for the good of God's kingdom here on earth."

They rocked in their chairs for a few moments in silence except for the low rumble of the waterfall in the distance. Mac continued with his instruction, "Really, it is up to you. Like I said earlier, you have to want to change. Even in wanting it, it will be difficult for you to do it on your own."

"You mean I can't do it myself?" Tommy asked. "Can't you just tell me a book to read? Who would I get to help me accomplish this change I need?"

"You know, Brother Sean leads a men's group that meets weekly for Bible study. They read the upcoming Sunday's passages and talk about how to incorporate those messages into their lives, and how to grow closer to Christ. That'd be a good place for you to start.

"Besides, it'll take some time for you to learn how to maintain that joy in all the various circumstances of life. But that's okay, because like the door, even while being repaired, you can still work. And this is the important part, Tommy—you need to keep working, to open up and let people in."

"I don't think I'm ready for that," Tommy said.

Mac pressed, "Tommy, everyone is broken to one degree or another. If we wait until we're in perfect repair, we would never invite others into relationship with us. The truth is, we will never be perfect—not in this life. In fact, waiting to be perfect can become an obstacle, a hindrance to our doing what we are called to do. We'd be denying others the chance to encounter Christ within us, like you just encountered Christ in those kids down there. Joy is contagious, and you just caught it. If we hide behind our imperfections, our brokenness, we'd miss out on the joy that is available to us."

"That was awesome, but I don't know about letting people other than Jess into my life," Tommy said. He crossed his legs and folded his arms.

Mac explained further, "Ah, but this is what we're called to, Tommy; to invite people into our lives, even in our brokenness. And in spite of our weakness, maybe even because of it, they will see the love of Jesus within us. And it is through the love of Jesus in us that we bring them to God."

"Isn't that the Church's job?" Tommy asked.

"If you mean the clergy," Mac said, "too many think so. But who is the Church, really, but us? We are the Church."

"What do you mean, 'we are the Church?'" Tommy asked.

"Almost everybody thinks of the Church as the building. But what would the building be without the people worshiping inside it? And the clergy can't do everything. There's just not enough of them. Their job is to lead their parishioners, to teach and to train them to go out into the community and serve God by serving others."

Hmm. This is too much. How will I ever... Tommy was overwhelmed by this new definition of the Church and his role in it. He thought a good Catholic was one who went to Mass on Sundays and holy days of obligation, and put money in the plate. Mac made it sound like he had all this extra work to do ...*invite people into my life, much less serve them? Sell them, maybe...*

"I think I see," he said slowly.

"And Tommy, this work is an ongoing process. Just as the weather beats on this old house, so the rain of selfishness, the wind of worldly concerns, the brutal cold and the relentless heat of lustful thoughts will always beat on your door. That's why you must be confident in the unreserved love of God, and surround yourself with those who love you and want the best for you and will help you repair your house."

Tommy listened intently to all the wisdom Mac shared. He felt like he was sitting at the knee of a master.

"One last thing," Mac said. "Once you start down this path, know that you will be tested."

"What do you mean?" Tommy asked.

"Remember, I said this change will be hard. It will take some time."

"Yes, I remember. So?"

"You will need to be prepared for when you encounter people with whom you've dealt in the past. They'll remember the old Tommy. They'll push you. They'll question your motives."

Tommy thought of the people he dealt with most every day. *Smitty won't know what to think. Kris won't believe it. And Bull...oh man...*

"But if you hold fast, once they see that your conversion is genuine, they'll come around. In fact, they'll be drawn to the inner beauty that is Christ within you. You'll give them the chance to experience God's awesome love and grace through you. You'll bring heaven to them."

Squeals of laughter floated up from the camp. The mid-afternoon sun dominated the brilliant blue sky. A hint of smoke mixed with the scent of evergreen filtered through the air, the best aromas of autumn.

"What about the house?" Tommy asked. "Are you going to sell it?"

"No."

"But why? You know that my offer..."

Mac lifted a hand to stop the protest.

"Three hundred thousand..." Tommy tried again, but a reassuring gleam in Mac's emerald eyes brought a sense of peace and calmness back to him.

"No, Tommy. I'm not going to sell this old place. But I am going to give it to you," Mac said.

"That's more than..." Tommy's jaw fell into his lap, "What'd you say?"

"That's right. I've already had the papers drawn. All you have to do is sign them and file them with the county."

"But you can't...I don't know..." Tommy's open-palmed hands shifted from side to side, surrendering in a shrug.

Mac got up from his chair, stretched and shuffled over to the railing. He watched the kids below file onto the school busses. Tommy joined him, "What is that place?"

"That's Camp Sparrow, a camp for special needs children," Mac told him. "They do a great service for kids with physical and mental challenges."

"Mac, I really don't know what to say." Mac and Tommy watched a couple of squirrels play chase up and around the pine trees. They ran out to the tip of a branch until it sagged so much it seemed it would break. But, just in time, they jumped to a leafless maple tree nearby and scampered away.

"I hear they're struggling to stay open," Mac said. They watched the busses drive off the grounds.

Tommy rubbed his eyes. "The beauty of this place; the valley nestled between the mountains, the church steeple across the way, the waterfall—is this heaven?"

Mac put his arm around Tommy and pulled him close. "Heaven is living in the presence of God."

Thirteen

Wednesday, November 21: Thanksgiving Eve

The Porsche zipped down GA Highway 60 to Dahlonega. The unkempt man in a familiar tattered plaid shirt stood on the shoulder of the highway holding a sign. It read, "Welcome Home." The fellow's grin caught Tommy's attention as he flew by. *Strange. Very strange.*

"I know what I'm gonna do," Tommy said out loud to himself. "This'll surprise the heck out of 'em. Can I make it before the store closes?" He found the Home Depot with a virtually empty parking lot. A dozen deep-fryer rigs stood unsold outside the entrance. A chalkboard announced their price had been slashed to half of what they were the day before. He left the Porsche at the curb, ran inside the store, and grabbed the first clerk he could find, "Y'all have those small heaters that'll fit underneath desks in stock?"

"Umm...I'm sure...a few at least," the young clerk said.

"Great!" Tommy rubbed his hands together. "I need to see a manager."

After a few minutes of consultation, he got back in his car and drove leisurely to his office in Roswell. The cell phone rang as he exited GA 400 at Holcomb Bridge Road. "Awesome. I'm almost there. Meet you in five."

Tommy burst into his office door exclaiming, "I can't believe how cold you keep it in here."

Rosemary shot out of her chair, finger wagging at Tommy, about to opine about his office management skills. She stopped short when she saw a man in an orange shirt hold the door open while another young man wearing a bibbed apron in the same bright orange hauled in a hand truck full of space heaters.

"Over here, boys," Tommy called to them. He waited in front of the cubicles in the bull pit. "Everybody listen up."

Ellen padded over to side with the property relations people. "What's this about?" one of the staff asked her in a low whisper. She shrugged her shoulders and pushed a few wayward strands of thin brown hair behind her ears. Bull stood in his office doorway, popping M&Ms.

Tommy had everyone's attention, "I know it's not Christmas, but I have a little present for you. Hand 'em out, will you, boys?"

The Home Depot employees began to deposit under-desk heaters at each work station. Sounds of ripping tape and Styrofoam rubbing against cardboard rose from the cubicle area. A chorus of "Thank you, Mr. Kennedy" rang out from the staff.

"And that's another thing," Tommy said. "Let's loosen up a little. From now on, please call me Tommy."

Ellen leaned against a blue-gray partition, her arms wrapped around her waist, mouth broadening into a smile. The Home Depot men collected the empty boxes and left.

"Oh, yeah. One more thing," Tommy called out. "The office will be closed on Friday. Everyone have a great Thanksgiving holiday with your family."

Rosemary clapped her hands together and raised them to her mouth as she lifted her eyes upward. She practically skipped back to her desk. Bull tossed in another M&M, turned on his heel, and went back to work.

"What's gotten into you?" Ellen asked on her way back to her office.

"I have something to tell you." Tommy followed her to her desk.

Ellen stepped around the desk and turned towards Tommy. Her glasses sat snuggly on the bridge of her nose. She put her hands on the pudge above her hips, "Well?"

"Sit down. Sit down." Tommy tapped on her desk. He was practically bouncing out of his shoes, grinning from ear to ear. He wadded a piece of paper into a ball and took a shot at the wastebasket behind Ellen's desk. "Darn!"

"What is it?" Ellen asked, smiling up at Tommy's infectious grin and schoolboy antics.

"I bought the camp," burst from Tommy's lips.

"The camp? What?"

"Or rather, I will buy it. Camp Sparrow off Wahsega Road. Don't you and Alex go there sometimes?"

"Uh...Yeah...How do you know about that?"

Tommy practically gushed as he told Ellen a condensed version of his encounter with Mac McCarter.

"Mac is giving me the property. Giving! Can you believe it? I can't. And it abuts Camp Sparrow. I was drawn to the place, the kids. The joy and wonderment I saw in those kids—it was overwhelming. I can't explain how I felt. That's when it hit me that that's where you go with Alex on those field trips."

Ellen confirmed, "They have an arrangement with Riverside Academy and other schools for special needs kids. But I'm afraid they're gonna have to shut down."

"Not anymore, they won't," Tommy promised. "I'll work on it Friday. I'll contact them, figure out a way to keep them operating. I'll be Big John to them."

"Big John?"

"Never mind. Anyway, I don't say this enough, but thank you for all your hard work and dedication. I can't imagine how difficult it must be as a single mom." He walked over to her side of the desk and pulled her up into a hug.

Surprised by his forcefulness, her glasses crashed into his chest. She removed them with one hand and with the other, tentatively returned the gesture.

Tommy prolonged the embrace, "I've been oblivious." He rocked her gently.

Ellen clasped her hands behind Tommy's back

"The way I treat the employees. How I've taken you for granted. Things will be better—I'll be better. You hold me to it."

After a moment, Ellen relaxed as she melted into Tommy. She struggled to maintain her composure. A tear left a wet spot on the pocket of his shirt. "Thank you, Tommy," she whispered.

Thursday, November 22: Thanksgiving afternoon

Tommy drove over to Bocca's Restaurant. Out of habit, he pulled the Porsche into a parking spot right in front of the entryway, paying no attention to its being for handicapped drivers. The maitre d' started toward the car to open the door, but then Tommy put the car in reverse and eased out. *What am I thinking?* He rolled down his window, "I'll be right back."

He drove next door to a shopping center and parked around the far side. The pent-up enthusiasm he felt put such a spring in his gate as he strode back to the restaurant, it was like he was walking on the moving sidewalk at the airport. Tommy had to stop a minute and force himself to take a deep breath to calm down. "Do you have a reservation?" the maitre d' asked when he entered the reception area.

"No. No. Just me."

"Table for one, then?" The scent of roasted garlic emanating from the kitchen titillated the senses. They agreed that Tommy would have a table in a corner of the bar area. From that vantage point, he could see who came and went, but unless a patron was specifically going to the bar, Tommy's table was safely obscure.

A young man dressed in a white tuxedo shirt with a skinny black bowtie and black pants asked if he wanted a drink and offered him a menu. "I'll have a scotch. Wait. You know what? Give me a water and a minute to look at the wine list."

It wasn't long before Jess arrived with Clare and Kathryn. The waiter appeared at just that time and stood in

Tommy's line of sight. "Did you decide on a wine, *signore*?" he asked with a light Italian accent.

"I'll have a glass of your Barolo Monfortino. No, a bottle. Bring the 2002," Tommy said.

"An excellent year," the waiter said.

"Do me a favor, buddy. Have the maitre d' come see me."

"Yes, *signore*." Tommy watched the waiter whisper to the maitre d' and point in his direction. The young man then hustled across to the main dining room.

In the middle of the main dining room sat sixteen four-top tables draped in fine white linen, each with a lit candle in the center. Booths lined the side walls. Built-in racks cradled hundreds of bottles of wine along the back wall.

A hostess escorted Jess's party to a table next to the serving station. Kathryn protested, "Can we have a table at the other end of the room? If you don't mind."

"Oh my goodness, Mother," Jess said.

"Really, Jessica, I don't see why, with all the empty tables we passed, they have to seat us next to all this noise and distraction," Kathryn defended herself.

Once seated, a waiter and a busboy appeared immediately, "May I tell you of our specials?" the waiter asked in a weak Italian imitation while the busboy filled the water glasses. "Of course, we have the traditional Thanksgiving dinner of turkey with cornbread dressing."

"Can I have a turkey leg?" Clare asked.

Jess glared her into quiet, and the waiter continued, "But if you're willing to be a little adventurous, the chef has prepared a prime rosemary-encrusted leg of lamb roasted to perfection. It pairs well with the very side dishes you will want for your Thanksgiving meal—candied bourbon yams, creamed spinach with artichoke hearts, green beans sautéed with garlic, fennel and leaks. And of course, this is Bocca; you can have a plate of pasta on the side of that."

"Mmm, it all sounds delicious," Jess said.

"And may I suggest our baked oysters as an appetizer?"

The busboy brought fresh hot bread for the table, placed a butter tray next to it, and poured olive oil into three saucers. He then asked, "Cracked pepper?"

An hour later, the maitre d' signaled Tommy. He took a last sip of wine, dabbed a napkin to his mouth, and followed the man behind the bar and into the kitchen. Jess's waiter met them at the door to the dining room.

"Oh my Lord," Kathryn said under her breath.

"What is it, Mother?" Jess asked.

"Don't look now, but Tommy is following behind our waiter." He pushed the dessert cart loaded with tiramisu, amaretto cheesecake, and a variety of cannoli. And of course, the cart carried pecan and pumpkin pies.

"Daddy's here?" Clare asked as she began to wriggle out of her chair.

Jess grabbed her, "You sit right there, young lady. Yes, Daddy is coming over to our table right now," she said between clenched teeth. Her eyebrows furrowed. Clare quaked in her seat, sitting on her hands.

"Ladies, may I present dessert?" the waiter asked. He began to describe the choices.

"What is this?" Jess asked, ignoring the dessert presentation. "What are you doing here?"

The waiter carried on, "...and Bocca's signature home-made tiramisu. And being Thanksgiving, we have..."

Tommy interrupted the waiter, "By any chance, do you have Bananas Foster?"

"Yes, *signore*, we do. We prepare it tableside."

Tommy looked to Jess, "Well?" Jess softened. Kathryn rolled her eyes. He turned to the waiter, "Let's have that and cappuccino all around—except a hot chocolate for the young lady."

"Right away, *signore*."

Jess was about to express her anger at his unannounced presence, but Tommy interceded, "Jess, may I speak, please?"

Clare couldn't stand it anymore. She popped off her seat and wrapped her arms around one of Tommy's legs. "Hey, sweat pea." He scooped her up into a hug. "Let me sit in your chair and talk to Mommy, okay?"

"Okay." Clare climbed into the seat next to Kathryn and whispered to her, "Daddy loves Mommy."

"Jess, I have been such a fool and I am so sorry. You know all that." Tommy took Jess's hand into both of his and looked deeply into her eyes. "I love you. I need you. I can't live without you."

"Oh, brother," Kathryn muttered.

"Hush, Mother," Jess said. She was entranced by Tommy's gaze.

"Kathryn has a right to be skeptical," Tommy said. "I've hurt you, and she wants to protect her daughter."

Kathryn raised her wine glass in a toast to that truth, took a sip, and then sat back in her chair and folded her arms.

"But I love you," Tommy said. "I love Clare. I love Kathryn."

"Humph" came from across the table.

"Okay, I respect your mother." He stared urgently into Jess's eyes. "I know you said you forgive me, but I beg you..."

Jess tilted her head, *He's never begged. And when's the last time I've heard him say the word 'love'? There's something about...What's he doing?*

Tommy got down on a knee, "Please. I need us to be family. I want to come home."

"Yes!" Jessica said and they stood as she flung her arms around Tommy. A few of the surrounding patrons clapped lightly. Jess and Tommy looked around, a light shade of red rising in their cheeks, and then they kissed. The waiter arrived with the Bananas Foster ensemble and the busboy delivered the coffees. They watched the spectacle—Clare from Tommy's lap. She squealed with delight when the liqueur was set aflame.

Dinner over, they all walked out of the restaurant, Jess and Tommy arm in arm, Tommy holding Clare's hand, "You want to ride with Daddy?"

Clare looked up at Jess, question marks for eyes.

"It's okay with me," Jess said.

Tommy headed toward the strip mall, Clare skipping along.

"So *that's* where you parked," Jess said.

Friday, November 23: Nighttime

The varsity cheerleaders wore white turtlenecks under their uniform vests to ward off the late November chill. This meant that Caroline, as a JV cheerleader, had on a green turtleneck, which coordinated nicely with the green of the St. L emblem on her chest and the green ribbon in her sandy blonde hair. She, along with the other JV cheerers, took their place in the student section on the first row of bleachers behind the team.

The band marched out onto the field, led by their drum line, which rapped out a catchy beat to help keep everyone's step in time. The varsity cheerleaders held a paper "Beat the Bulldogs" banner at the goalpost, while the band formed two lines for the team to run through on their way to the sideline. JT and all the senior players burst through the sign as the band played the Knights' fight song. Excitement and tension filled the air, as this quarterfinal contest against the SEG Consolidated Bulldogs was evenly matched.

JT found his mom in the stands sitting with Br. Sean. Br. Sean retained his position as athletic director at St. Laurence, but he had retired from the gridiron a few seasons before. JT looked to either end of the stadium, and then back to Kellie. She answered his questioning look with a shrug of her shoulders.

The game got off to its expected start. Neither team was able to sustain a drive that achieved more than two first downs. With five minutes left to play in the second quarter, there was still no score. St. Laurence had the ball, second and eight at the Bulldog forty. A pass play was called and JT's route was a ten-yard and out. A perfect spiral hit him in the hands; yet he dropped the ball. His shoulders slumped and toes dragged the turf as his momentum carried him past the sidelines after the play. His hands covered his face mask, hiding an "oh-no" look in his eyes.

Then, JT saw his dad watching from the fence beyond the track. Tommy clapped and called out encouragement, "C'mon, son. Focus. You can do it."

JT's posture inflated. He gave his dad a subtle fist-pump from the waist. He hustled back to the huddle. The next play was the familiar 44 power. The signals were called, the snap and then the handoff to the back-side back. JT blocked down on the defensive tackle, and when the fullback joined in the double team, JT peeled off and sealed the inside of the line. The Knights picked up the first down and the drive was alive. A few more power plays and inside dives, and the Knights found themselves at the nine-yard line with less than a minute to play in the half. The Bulldogs stacked the line, expecting St. Laurence to try to plow their way into the end zone. Sure enough, another 44 power play was called. Except this time, the quarterback pulled the ball from the running back's belly, while JT darted past the linebackers. An easy toss found him all alone—touchdown Knights!

Pandemonium broke out in the stands. Kellie threw herself into Br. Sean's arms. The band struck up the fight song. Tommy thrust his fists triumphantly into the air. JT trotted to the sideline, ball in hand, pointing at the fence.

"Who's he pointing to?" Kellie asked.

"I think that's Tommy down there," Br. Sean said. "It sure is. Tommy, my boy."

During intermission, Br. Sean stopped at the fence on his way back from the concession stand, balancing a tray of popcorn bags and Coke cups. "Come and join us, Tommy." He nodded his head in Kellie's direction. "I bought enough for you, too."

Tommy saw three bags and Cokes. "I don't know, Brother Sean. Kellie would probably rather I didn't." He looked up to where she was in the stands. She waved hello and another wave to come on up.

"I'm glad you're here," Kellie told him as she took a Coke from Br. Sean. "We saw you down at the fence after JT caught that touchdown pass."

"Yeah, what a response after he missed that easy catch at the sidelines," Tommy crowed. "Did you see the way he steamrolled the tackle on those 44 power plays during that drive?"

"Reminded me of old times," Br. Sean said, slapping Tommy on the back.

"Hi, Daddy." Caroline came up and gave her daddy a hug. She took his cup of Coke from him.

"Have some," Tommy invited.

She took a big gulp and handed it back to him with a sly smile, and then scampered away to rejoin the cheerleaders.

"Jess and Clare not with you?" Kellie asked.

"Not tonight," Tommy said. "She thought it'd be better for me to come by myself."

"Well, she's perfectly welcome," Kellie said as she tried to stuff too many pieces of popcorn in her mouth. A few escaped and bounced off her chin and floated down into her lap.

"That's graceful," Tommy said and all three of them broke into laughter.

"You know, Tommy is this year's sponsor for our annual Thanksgiving Community Dinner tomorrow," Br. Sean told Kellie.

"Really?" Kellie said. "Tommy, that's wonderful."

"Say, Tommy my boy, a thought just hit me," Br. Sean said. "How about you joining in with our men's Bible study?"

Tommy's eyes widened. *Where'd that come from?* "Funny, a friend recently suggested I do something like that," Tommy said, and he looked up at the night sky beyond the stars. "Maybe I will."

The second half continued the grudge match similar to the first. Thankfully, the scoreboard at the end of the game showed 14 to 3 in favor of the Knights. Tommy excused himself and headed down to the field.

Amidst the players, coaches, cheerleaders, and fans, Tommy found JT in the crowd, walked right up to him, and in a big bear hug, lifted JT's feet off the ground. "What a game! You played great, son."

"Thanks, Dad," JT said. They stood there in awkward silence until the coach called them to gather around him for the after-game team huddle.

The coach's final comments focused on JT, "...and for his dominance of their D-line that allowed us to churn out a victory, the game ball goes to JT Kennedy." All the players cheered on their captain as he received the honor. The coach then led them in a closing prayer.

"I'm proud of you, son," Tommy said after the team was dismissed.

Classmates and cheerleaders swarmed up to JT with high fives and back pats. "Good game. Way to go." They pulled JT away from Tommy, leaving him on the edge of the crowd. He shoved his hands into his pockets and shuffled his feet when he caught the coach nodding his way while in conversation with a gentleman dressed in a black trench coat with a yellow and black scarf. He waved Tommy over.

"Let me introduce Tommy Kennedy, JT's dad," the coach said to the man. "Mr. Kennedy, this is Sam Johns. He's a scout for Georgia Tech."

"Mr. Kennedy, what a pleasure to meet you," said Mr. Johns. "I remember your days as a Yellow Jacket. Too bad you blew out your knee."

"Yeah, well. It happens," Tommy shrugged.

"We're very interested in your son," Sam Johns said.

"That's awesome," Tommy said. "If I may brag a little, did you see that drive at the end of the first half?"

"That was the turning point of the game," Coach added. "It was like JT caught fire and got the entire team revved up."

"Very impressive," the scout agreed. "Your son is quite a leader on the field."

"And off," Coach said.

Tommy spied JT in a crowd of players heading for the field house. "Excuse me, gentlemen." He trotted toward them and called, "JT. Son, wait up."

JT carried his helmet by the facemask as it supported his shoulder pads. He stopped and turned around.

"Son. Hey, I wanted to talk with you a minute."

"'Sup, Dad."

"I know I've been absent. If it's okay with you, I'd like to plug in again, be around more."

"Sure, Dad. Whatever." JT turned back toward the field house.

"No, wait. Really, JT. I want to be more involved."

JT's shoulders rose and fell in a visible exhale. "Next week, we'll be at home for the semi's."

"I don't mean just for the games," Tommy said. He cleared his throat, "Listen, JT. You don't owe me or anything. But I just wanted to tell you I'm sorry."

"Sure. Okay," JT said, and he again attempted to head to the locker room.

Tommy caught him on the arm, "Son, please." Tommy's eyes locked with JT's. A film of tears thickened across his eyes. "Give me a chance."

JT's head cocked a little to the side. The space between his brows crinkled.

"What about tomorrow?" Tommy pressed.

"Tomorrow? Well, you know. Practice in the morning. And then the annual Community Dinner for the needy families in town after that. The team has to serve at the dinner."

"How 'bout I join in with you?" Tommy offered.

"Sure...I guess," JT said. "You want to work at the dinner?"

"Other parents help out, don't they?"

"Uh...yeah. But you haven't..."

"We'll be together. Do some good for the school and help the poor. It'll be fun."

"Uh...sure. Practice is at 9."

Tommy reached up and grabbed JT behind the neck and pulled him in for another hug. "That's great, son. Thank you." Over JT's shoulder he could see Kellie, enfolded in Br. Sean's arms, smiling down at them.

Br. Sean pointed with a victory salute at the father and son on the field, "Tommy, my boy!"

The end.

End Note

Hello, and thank you for reading The Broken Door. My name is Brian Pusateri, and I'm the founder of Broken Door Ministries. Let me share a little about how our ministry and this book came about.

My pastor gave me the book Unbound: A Practical Guide to Deliverance by Neal Lozano. I read that book while on a silent retreat in the fall of 2011. Kneeling in front of the Blessed Sacrament at 3 a.m. while on that retreat, I heard God speak to my heart, "Brian, like you just read in the book, if you want to break free of the chains that bind you and find peace, you need to tell others about the areas of recurring sin in your life."

From that experience was born 4thdayletters.com, a weekly blog about the struggles I and all of us face in our daily walk with God. One particular post came flooding into my head which I named *The Parable of the Broken Door.*

I asked my friend and author Joe Galloway to help me edit that entry. As we discussed it, I made an off-hand remark about there being a book in there somewhere. Well, Joe and I may have dismissed that comment as happenstance or coincidental. But I believe there are no coincidences, only "God-incidents." It wasn't long before God touched Joe's heart with the entire story line while he drove a lonely stretch of interstate.

I hope the message of the book touches your heart as well. And the message is this: We are all broken in some way. My brokenness was years of unchaste behaviors, which began after I was molested by a priest as a young boy. We all disguise our brokenness behind masks of our own making, masks that hide the shame and embarrassment we feel. Like most people, my recurring sins were known to no one other than me and my confessor. I was blessed to have a wonderful wife and family along with a strong faith and active church involvement. This provided a façade to hide behind. But still, I had my secret. My recurring sinfulness worked to continually cloud my relationship with God.

But the good news is that there is hope. Hope in the healing power of Jesus' unconditional and unrelenting love. Broken Door Ministries exists to help Christians recognize that we are loved even as we are "broken doors." And in that love, and through our brokenness, we are called to share Christ with others.

Do you deal with recurring sin? Do you cover it up with excuses, masks, and façades? Are you walled in by shame and tired of living in falsehood? Truthfulness about our struggles allows the light of Christ to reach even the darkest corners of our souls and permits healing to begin.

If you are interested in breaking free from recurring sin and want to learn more about how that freedom comes from the crucified Christ, subscribe to www.4thdayletters.com. If you want to help others overcome their struggles with recurring sin, invite Broken Door Ministries to speak at your church or meeting. Do that at http://brokendoorministries.com.

I suffered and carried this cross of sin alone for 47 years. Please don't let that happen to you or anyone you love. This ministry is dedicated to helping others avoid that mistake. May God bless you and yours.

Brian

About the Author

Joe Galloway lives in Greenville, South Carolina, but he's from New Orleans and misses real po-boys on good French bread. In fact, it was while driving down to the Big Easy to meet up with his wife, Charleen, for her father's funeral that this story came to him like a deluge. He had to wake his teenage daughter, pull over, and have her drive so that he could write out the outline and synopsis between Montgomery and Mobile.

By day in the Upstate, Joe works as a Financial Advisor. He strives to grow perfect tomatoes and enjoys the week-long struggle to complete the *Wall Street Journal* crossword puzzle.

Made in the USA
Columbia, SC
05 September 2017